*A
Harlequin
Romance*

OTHER
Harlequin Romances
by HILARY WILDE

THE SWEET SPRING

by

HILDA NICKSON

HARLEQUIN BOOKS   TORONTO
WINNIPEG

Original hard cover edition published in 1972
by Mills & Boon Limited, 17-19 Foley Street,
London W1A 1DR, England

© Hilda Nickson 1972

Harlequin edition published December 1972

SBN 373-01647-6

Printed in Canada

1647

CHAPTER I

The morning held a promise of spring. Her hand on the door handle of her small car Melanie paused for a moment and gazed down at the familiar view. The wooded valley where during the daylight hours nestled in secret a small housing estate, showing after dark a twinkle of lights like a young girl wearing her first jewels, while on the perimeter the crooked spire of Chesterfield's parish church looked unselfconsciously down. It was a view which was an intimate part of her life and bound tightly with her love for her home. She had been born here in this rambling old house. She could not imagine living anywhere else—though she supposed there would come a time when she would marry and have a home of her own.

A shadow crossed her face. Somehow, the kind of love she wanted seemed a long time coming. Or did she expect too much of the men with whom she had met and become friendly? It was not that she craved marriage exactly. She led a busy life. But more and more often these days she found herself envying the kind of love which still existed between her parents. That special relationship which surpassed all others—an exclusive *belonging*.

A tap on the dining room window brought her out of her reverie. It was her mother, who now pushed up the casement window.

'Darling—you're going to be late.'

'I'm just going, Mother. It's such a lovely morning—'

She slid behind the wheel of her car. Unless the townbound traffic was thinner than usual this morning she would already be a few minutes late opening their book-and-music shop. Normally she and her father

5

travelled to town together, but he was still convalescing from an illness and at present was only going to the shop to help out on busy days.

The journey to town took only a quarter of an hour. Melanie parked her car and made her way to Knife-smith's Gate where their shop was situated. It was a prosperous business, occupying two sides of a corner and extending to several ordinary-sized shops. Melanie could see the sign as she walked along the street. R. Lawrence & Son. Why did one never see *&* *Daughter*? she wondered wryly. She had taken the place of a son ever since she had left school.

Out of pride mingled with sentiment, and looking optimistically into the future, her father had had that sign painted when her brother Rory had been only one year old. Six months later Rory had died as a result of some sudden infant infection. Melanie had been trying to be both son and daughter to her parents ever since, forgoing not only a university education but, in an effort to make up for their disappointment and loss, a secret ambition to be a professional pianist.

As she expected, a group of assistants waited outside for her to unlock the premises. She smiled and offered an apology for her lateness as a matter of courtesy, but as she put her key in the lock her attention was arrested by a tall man looking in the window. A customer at this hour on a Monday morning? But it was his profile and general bearing which arrested her attention. He had the most interesting and intelligent face she had ever seen. There was both strength and refinement in the lines of his mouth and jaw, and a certain dignity in the set of his shoulders, which denoted him a man of standing, of importance. He glanced at his watch, then looked swiftly in her direction, and feeling suddenly embarrassed at being caught scrutinising him she averted her gaze quickly and pushed open the door. There had been implied criticism in his glance. She was almost five minutes late in opening the shop. If he were an employer, she felt certain this was one of the things he would not tolerate.

But it was quite absurd to make speculations like this about a perfect stranger. He was not even a regular customer. She had never seen him before.

She collected the mail from the letter box behind the door, passed inside the shop and went through to the office situated in the book department. The man was probably not even a potential customer. She was imagining things this morning. Forget him.

But as it happened that wasn't too easy. After glancing swiftly through the letters she went into the shop, and there he was in the non-fiction department. She managed to retreat without his seeing her, and a few minutes later he was gone.

'An early customer,' she remarked to Peter Lee, the senior assistant in that department. 'Did he buy anything?'

'A book on local history. He asked for a couple on the Peak District by name—which we hadn't got.'

'He would. You had heard of them, I hope?'

'I hadn't, as a matter of fact.'

'But you didn't say so.'

'Not likely, especially to one of his type.'

Melanie smiled faintly. 'I'm glad you're able to sum up the customers so well.'

Peter grinned. 'It comes with practice. I looked the titles up in the catalogue and offered to get them for him.'

'He's ordered them?' Peter nodded. 'Then order half a dozen of each. They must be good if someone like that asks for them. He's on an early holiday, I shouldn't wonder. I've never seen him before, have you?

In a business like this, though one naturally did not know every customer by name, one became familiar with faces.

7

'No, he's a stranger to me, too,' Peter said. 'But I shouldn't think he's on holiday or he wouldn't have ordered them.'

'Did he say he wanted them urgently?'

'No, and he didn't ask how long it would take.'

Melanie thought for a moment. 'I think I'll ring round one or two of our friends—see if any of them have got copies to spare. I wouldn't like to be found wanting by a man like that. What name did he give, by the way?'

Peter consulted his order book. 'Hamilton. D. K. Hamilton.'

Melanie wondered what the initials stood for. David Kenneth? Donald Keith? Douglas—what else? There weren't many names beginning with K. Kurt? Yes, that would just about suit him, she decided. But what was she doing, thinking this way? She didn't know the man. She was beginning to think she must have spring fever. She applied herself to her work, but half way through the morning she thumbed idly through the telephone book looking down the Hamiltons. There wasn't anyone with exactly those initials, however, and after a minute or two she slammed the directory shut. This was ridiculous. Why was she so curious about this man? Curiosity was all it could be. She couldn't possibly be attracted to him. She had no lack of masculine company. She had quite a number of men friends.

She was almost beginning to resent the man!

She was glad that evening that her parents were having some friends in to dinner and music and had asked her to play the piano for them. Perhaps then she could forget about this D. K. Hamilton who had disturbed her so much. Most of her parents' friends were musical, and she knew it would be an enjoyable evening. During dinner, however, there was some very disturbing conversation. It seemed the local council had been given the go-ahead on a new motorway, and all kinds of rumours were going around on where this would be sited.

' As I see it,' one of the guests were saying, ' there are only two places where it *could* go. One is straight through that line of cottages down by Mill Lane, and the other is—across your valley and right through your sitting room.'

Richard Lawrence saw his wife's colour fade, then a tiny pulse began to beat in her throat.

' Don't worry, Helen,' he said soothingly. ' There'll be a lot of wild rumours flying about before the site is finally decided upon. Anyway, it would be much too expensive to cross the valley. They'd have to build a bridge right across.' Helen shuddered at the idea. ' My dear, Harry wouldn't even have mentioned it if he'd thought there was the remotest possibility,' Richard said.

To Melanie, too, it did not even bear thinking about. A motorway across ' their ' lovely valley, or anywhere near the house would be terrible. The motor car was indeed taking over.

After dinner, however, all was forgotten except music. Melanie was asked to play some Chopin which she loved, and for a little while she became as lost as her audience. Then her mother and father sang some Mimi and Rodolfo duets from ' La Bohème ', and the evening flew on enchanted wings as first one beautiful piece of music was played or sung, and then another.

To Melanie's delight the two books she had located by telephoning a Sheffield bookseller were delivered by post the following afternoon. She smiled to herself and left them on her desk. She would hand them to Mr D. K. Hamilton herself. It would be interesting to see the undoubted surprise on his face, especially if he came into the shop in a few days' time. Disappointingly, however, he did not, and Melanie felt she had wasted both time and effort in getting the books for him so promptly. He was probably quite well aware how long it took to get books on order and would not even bother to come into the shop again for at least ten days—even a fortnight. After four or five days had elapsed she shrugged off the subject of Mr Hamilton and his books. But then quite suddenly she came face to face with him upstairs in the music department.

'Oh, Mr Hamilton,' she said at once, 'your books have arrived.'

At first his face showed no expression at all. He stared at her as if she were a being from another world.

'My books?' he repeated at last.

'Yes, the two you ordered.' She repeated the titles. Another hard stare. Then: 'Oh. Oh, I see. Then I'll collect them before I go.'

No surprise, barely any reaction at all. Not even a word of thanks. And it was only five days since he had ordered them. Certainly the ones they had ordered from the publisher had not yet arrived. Feeling slightly annoyed and regretting having spoken to him even, Melanie turned and went downstairs again. She took the books from her office and handed them to Peter.

'He'll be down for them presently,' she said. 'He's upstairs. I told him they'd arrived and he didn't show the slightest sign either of surprise or gratitude.'

Peter pulled a face. 'Some people are like that. He'd probably make a good poker player.'

'Maybe.'

But what an absolutely infuriating man he must be to live with. Why on earth had she gone to so much trouble for him? Any other customer wanting a book they didn't have in stock would have had to wait much longer. It was only in very rare cases that she tried to get a book from another bookseller. The next time she saw him, either in the shop or elsewhere, she would simply ignore him.

At that moment her father came into the office, and Melanie switched on the electric kettle to make mid-morning coffee. Richard Lawrence flung down an open newspaper on to the desk.

'Take a look at that, Melanie. It looks as though that proposed new motorway might cut right through our house, after all.'

'Oh, no, Father—'

'It's true.'

Melanie looked at the newspaper. A whole page had been taken up by maps and diagrams of proposed routes, subject to surveys. There was also a paragraph inviting anyone who had any objections to any route to send them to the local council.

'You'll send in an objection, of course.'

'Naturally—if it will make any difference,' answered her father, 'but wherever it goes it's bound to upset somebody. You could argue that those old cottages on Mill Lane would be better bulldozed, anyway, but they're home to somebody—quite a number of somebodies. And strictly speaking, I don't suppose they're much older than our house except that Hillrise has been kept in better condition.'

'Oh, but, Father, it's awful! I love our house and that view across the valley. So does Mother. She'll be frightfully upset.'

'I know. Me, too. I expect we'd get compensation, but that's not the point. That house holds so many memories for all of us. But, Melanie, try to put on a good face about it for your mother's sake. Even if the worst happens, it won't come about for a long time yet, so don't let's talk about it too much at home, eh? Not any more than we have to, if you know what I mean. If the worst *does* happen and we have to find a new house —well, there'll be plenty of time to get used to the idea, adjust our minds. In her off moments, your mother has often complained about the house being too big or too old, things of that sort. She hasn't meant them seriously, of course. They've only been little grumbles, but between us we could persuade her that we'd be *better* with a new house. And in a county like Derbyshire there are plenty of hills with as many views, though much further out of town, of course.'

Melanie put a hand across his shoulder. 'I'll do my best.'

But she suppressed a pang of something like envy. Always, as long as she could remember, her father had shielded her mother from the hard knocks of life, the difficult decisions, the major worries, and had brought Melanie up to do the same. 'Don't make a noise, darling, it'll make Mummy's head ache.' 'Let's not tell Mummy about that, it will only worry her unnecessarily.' Or, 'Don't mention so-and-so to your mother until I've thought what to do about it.'

She did not want a man to shield herself in the same way exactly, but it would be nice to have someone on whom to lean occasionally, someone strong and reliable, someone perhaps like—

She pulled herself up as the name Hamilton came into her mind. She had liked the look of him, yes, but appearances could be deceptive, as she was beginning to discover quite quickly in this particular instance. It was all so ridiculous, anyway, she told herself. These kind of foolish romantic thoughts were not like her in the least. It *must* be the spring.

'Anyway,' she said, continuing her conversation with her father, 'it may never happen. We shall just have to hope for the best.'

Richard Lawrence looked at her fondly. 'You're very attached to our old house, too, aren't you?'

She nodded. 'It's the only home I've ever known, Father. That view—with the lights twinkling through the trees at night. And in the daylight, that friendly old crooked spire.'

'I know, I know. If we ever have to move, it will be a wrench for all of us. But when are you going to get married, Melanie? You'd have your own place then, wouldn't you? I mean—you'd have had to leave Hill-rise some time, unless you've made up your mind to remain single all your life. What about all those good-looking young men you've had at various times? Don't tell me none of them has ever asked you—'

'They were only friends, Father. Some of them might have had other ideas, but—'

'But what?'

'Oh—I don't know. Most of them seemed to have such a limited idea of love. I'd want to come first in a man's life, just as Mother comes first in yours, not be of secondary importance to a man's hobby or sport, or even his work. More likely of course the fault is in me. Perhaps I've never really been in love, perhaps I'm not capable of it.'

'Nonsense, my dear. You were always a very affectionate child. You've developed into a business woman now, of course, but you're capable of loving very deeply. Maybe none of the men you've met so far have appealed to you sufficiently. But you must remember this. Love deepens *after* marriage—if it's any good, that is—and goes on deepening. Love is doing things together, forgiving each other, loving the other so much that when he is miserable, you're miserable too, when he's happy, so are you, if one of you treads on a nail the other's foot hurts.'

'That's exactly the kind of love I'm looking for. I mean—not looking for exactly, but the kind I'd want.'

Richard Lawrence gave a slight shake of his head. 'You won't find it very easily, and it doesn't happen all at once. When you first realise you're in love, you think you couldn't possibly love each other any more, but that's only the beginning. Love is like wine—it takes time to mature and the more mature it is, the better its flavour. But it's your mother who should be telling you these things, not I.'

Melanie smiled and dropped a kiss on his forehead.

' I'll check up, see if she feels the same, but she might not be as eloquent as you, of course.' Then she added thoughtfully : ' Tell me, Father—are *men* romantic? In the same way that women are supposed to be, I mean.'

' I think they are underneath, though they might not show it. I think most men at heart are looking for a great love—those who haven't found it already, that is. Every man has his ideal, I'm sure of it. His ideal woman who has everything. Beauty, brains, charm, a capacity for loving—and that special something one can't explain.'

' That special something probably means love and devotion to *him*,' answered Melanie wryly. ' But I wonder how many men give any thought to how *they* measure up as a woman's ideal?' She thought of some of the men she had met—their demands on one's attention and emotions without giving the slightest consideration in return, their preoccupation with their own personal enjoyment, their own opinions, their own careers, their general falling short of any ideal she might have been harbouring.

' It works both ways, Melanie,' her father said. ' It's bound to.'

' I suppose so. I wonder—do men and woman *ever* find their ideal, or do they, in most instances, settle for something less?'

' I should think the majority don't even think about it. They fall in love and that's that. They get married and sort themselves out afterwards. Even the ones who are—shall we say—a little harder to please are probably not in the least conscious of having an ideal. They only know that first one, then another who looked as though they might be a life partner, falls short.'

' What makes people hard to please in that way?' Melanie wondered.

' Perhaps they're more intelligent than others, or more sensitive—or it could be that they expect too much.'

Melanie thought of this conversation a number of

times during the following weeks, but came to no definite conclusion about her own motives for the ideals she might hold about a future husband. How did one know whether or not one was intelligent or sensitive? How did one know whether one measured up to any man's ideal? Perhaps she was one of those who expected too much in the men she had met. Once, she found herself speculating on what type of woman was Mr D. K. Hamilton's ideal, and again tried to dismiss the man from her mind. She was having lunch one day, however, in a nearby restaurant, seated alone at a table for two, when he entered. He caught sight of her and walked across to her.

'Miss Lawrence?'

'Yes—' she answered uncertainly.

'I don't want to interrupt your lunch, but may I have a word with you?'

'Certainly. Perhaps you'd like to join me. I'm— not over-fond of eating alone, actually, but there are times when one has little option.'

He sat down and attracted the attention of a waitress. Melanie watched his face as briskly and without a trace of indecision he gave his order. He was clean-shaven, a fact which alone gave sharper edges to his features, and she judged his age to be between thirty and forty. He would almost certainly have a wife and family.

'I hope you don't mind my talking business,' he began while waiting for his soup, 'but I wanted to thank you for getting my books so promply. I understand you made a special effort.'

Melanie wondered how he had learned of that, and wished he hadn't.

'Not really,' she answered defensively. 'If I think a customer is in a hurry for a certain book, I do sometimes use an unorthodox method.'

'I wasn't in a hurry,' the aggravating man pointed out.

'I thought you might be—and you were a new customer. I wanted to make a good impression. Books do, unfortunately, take longer to arrive when one only orders single copies.'

'Oh, why is that?' he queried.

'It's a question of economics.'

He gave her a cold, darting glance. '*Economics.* We hear of nothing else these days.'

'It's sometimes justified,' Melanie answered tartly. 'Obviously, single copies—or even two—would have to be sent by mail, and postage charges are so high it would completely swallow the profit in most cases. Naturally, the distributor waits until he has enough orders to make up a sizeable parcel which can be sent by road.'

'I see. And you think those are good business methods,' he said flatly.

'I didn't say so. But one has to use common sense.'

'Of course,' he said, with a strong hint of sarcasm. Then he added, 'But if you can do it to impress a new customer—like me—why can't it be done every time?'

'It isn't as simple as that.' Not for anything, now, would she tell him how she had managed to get his books so promptly, and she hoped no one else had told him. It was a trade secret, and not practised by every bookseller by any means. 'Anyway, Mr Hamilton, why start by thanking me for getting your books so promptly, then end up by being critical?'

The waitress brought his main course, and he waited until he had been served with vegetables before answering.

'I was merely following a line of thought, Miss Lawrence, trying to understand the world of business. Yours looks quite a successful one, I might say.'

'Then there can't be much wrong with our methods, can there?' she retorted swiftly.

'That doesn't necessarily follow.'

Melanie's eyes became steely. He was probably implying that their charges were too high, and she felt that as he had all but thrust his company upon her, the least he could do was to be polite.

'Will you explain that remark, Mr Hamilton?' she asked icily.

But he met her challenge calmly. 'I was merely generalising, Miss Lawrence. Er—yours is a family business, I understand?'

'Yes, you could call it that—though my mother doesn't take an active part.'

'Just you and your brother and your father.'

She smiled faintly. 'I haven't a brother. I'm the "& Son".'

'Oh, I see—' he said slowly, as if that explained everything, though what, Melanie couldn't be sure.

To save him asking further questions, she explained a little further about her brother, though she did not go too deeply into the personal feelings of her parents, their disappointment or even her own desire to be both son and daughter.

'So actually, you're an only child?' came the almost inevitable question.

Melanie knew an all too familiar reaction. Her grey eyes glinted.

'Yes,' she answered, 'that's right. And before you make the usual comments, may I say that I am neither lonely, spoilt, indulged, nor do I have all my own way.'

His eyes widened. He paused, a piece of steak half way to his mouth. Then he answered: 'Neither do you show any signs of being shy or withdrawn.'

Melanie drew an angry breath, but fought down a desire to hit back once more. This man seemed to bring out the worst in her! She became aware that he was eying her closely and knew that she was being sized up by him. Then she relaxed. After all, she might have forestalled him unjustly.

'No, I'm not shy or withdrawn,' she answered

17

equably. 'I have been taught to mix with all kinds of people, and of course, in my job—'

He nodded, and Melanie detected a slight relaxing of his own expression.

'I suppose it's a sore point with you—this reaction by people when they discover you're an only child.'

'I'm afraid so, and I get rather fed up with it at times, though I don't normally hit back *before* they say anything.'

'We all have our off days. It's wrong of people to jump to conclusions about anyone, of course, and perhaps in particular about an only child. Some parents fall over backwards to prevent an only offspring being spoilt, and as a consequence are sometimes more strict than they might be.'

'*That* doesn't apply in my case, either,' she said firmly.

'Perhaps not, but I think you should allow that being the only child does often cause problems of one kind or another. Various frustrations, complexes—but sometimes a very high level of intelligence too, because an only child tends to read instead of playing games.'

'I used to play the piano,' Melanie said involuntarily.

'Used to?'

'When I was a child. I still do, of course.'

'There aren't so many who keep it up. Do you play well?'

'Fairly well, I think. You were in the music section one day when I spoke to you. Are you musical?'

'If you mean do I play an instrument—no, though I'm very fond of good music.'

Melanie thought this was at least one thing in his favour, and was glad that the topic of conversation had moved from herself. It was time, she thought, for *her* to ask a few questions.

'I noticed the books you ordered were about the Peak District, and Derbyshire in general. Are you new to the area?'

He nodded. 'Fairly. I come from the north—the Lake District.'

'Oh—lovely.'

'But this part of the country is equally lovely from what I've seen of it, and I think Chesterfield is a most interesting little town. Those narrow streets—at least, some of them are narrow—and the picturesque black and white timbered shops with those odd gables—some of them look almost like sets in a film. I should think the architecture is Elizabethan, isn't it?'

'A little before Elizabeth, actually. Tudor. In fact the church dates back to the fourteenth century.'

'Weird—that twisted spire. I'd heard about it before I came here, of course. It's almost as famous as the Leaning Tower of Pisa.'

She laughed. 'Well, not quite. But it's certainly a curiosity. We love it, of course. It spells home. Like Pisa, though, it was not built that way. It's due to a lack of proper cross-supports and the warping of wood under the expansion of the lead. The experts wanted to pull it down and rebuild it some hundred years ago, but I'm glad they didn't. As I said, it's a symbol of home to those of us who were born here. Have you done much exploring further afield? The Dales or places like Chatsworth and our other stately homes?'

He shook his head. 'Not yet. I—suppose I couldn't persuade you to act as my guide—say on Sunday week?'

The invitation was so unexpected she could only stare at him for a moment, wondering whether he was really serious.

'Well, I—a run out into the country is always very nice, of course,' she temporized.

'Then you will?'

'Yes,' she said, coming to a decision. On the whole she liked this man. He intrigued her. 'Yes, I don't think I'm doing anything that Sunday. Shall we say—

19

weather permitting? None of the houses will be open at this time of year, of course—it's too early—and there won't be much point in running out to the Dales or moors if it's too wet to get out and walk.'

'Very well. If the weather is impossible, perhaps we can make another date.' He looked at his watch. 'If you'll excuse me, I must be off. I have an appointment with someone at two, and it's nearly that already. Thank you for allowing me to sit and talk to you—and I shall hope for a fine day on Sunday week.'

He rose and signalled to the waitress for his bill. Melanie watched him depart, a smile of half amusement on her face. It should be quite stimulating getting to know this man, pitting her wits against his. At least he would not be boring.

On Sunday Melanie played several solo piano items at a charity concert, as she was often asked to do, and as she acknowledged the applause she thought she saw him sitting at the back of the hall, but when she searched the faces of the crowd later as coffee was being served, she did not see him. Perhaps she had been mistaken. It was ridiculous to suppose he would come to listen to her play, but she had to admit that she would have been enormously pleased if he had.

Something happened the following day, however, which put everything else right out of her mind. On this particular day she decided to run home to lunch as her mother would be at home alone, her father having gone to a booksellers' conference.

'Mother!' she called out as she came into the house. 'What on earth are those two caravans doing in the field just by the copse?'

'I don't know, dear. They were towed there about the middle of the morning. I went out about half past ten to do my shopping, and when I came back there they were.'

'Have you seen anyone?'

'A dark-haired young man, that's all.'

Melanie frowned. 'It's odd—at this time of the year.'

'It's odd at any time of the year. That's grazing land, not a camping ground.'

'Well, I expect they've got permission, whoever it is. And of course, Mr Thompson doesn't put his cattle out until next month. Maybe I'll take a little walk after lunch and try to find out something.'

The copse was actually part of the property of Hillrise. It was all that remained of a small wood and had been Melanie's childhood playground. At various times she had planted daffodils and primroses and other flowers; even now, she loved to walk beneath the trees. There was a gap in the hedge which separated the farmer's field from the copse, a gap kept open in days past by the passage of children, and later by Melanie as an adult, just wide enough for her to squeeze through, but not to admit the bulk of a cow. After lunch she put on an old jacket and scrambled through the opening. The caravans were very smart and modern, and one was bigger than the other. She walked slowly past the bigger one, but there was neither sound nor movement coming from within. But when she passed the smaller of the two she heard someone moving about, and as she came level with one of the windows the face of a man appeared. Melanie smiled and gave a friendly wave, hoping that this would bring him to the door—which it did.

'Hello,' he said. 'Taking a walk?'

'In a way. I live in the house there—Hillrise. Are you on holiday?'

He grinned. 'No such luck. I'm working around here. But I'm just having a coffee. Won't you join me?'

'Thank you.' Melanie stepped inside. 'It's my lunch hour, too, really, but I saw your caravan and couldn't resist coming to find out what was happening.'

'You're honest, anyway,' he said. 'And I like that.

What do you do?' He handed her a cup of coffee and invited her to sit down.

'My father has a book and music shop in town. Lawrence's. Do you know it?'

He nodded. 'I was in there the other day buying some records. Not that I can use them in here. I have to rely on my transistor when I'm in.' He gave a quick smile. 'So you're Miss Lawrence and you help your father with the business.'

'Melanie,' she told him. 'What's your name?'

'Eric. Eric Eaton.'

'And what are you doing here? Do you live in the area?'

He shook his head. 'I'm from Caldwell, a little place way on the other side of Derby, and I'm here to do some surveying. I'm a civil engineer.'

'*Oh no!*'

'What's the matter?'

She stared at him. 'The matter? You're the one who decides where this proposed new motorway is going to run, aren't you? Do you realise that our house might have to come down?'

'Whew! I'm sorry, I didn't realise. Anyway, nothing's settled, you know. We've got to survey a very large area. Because we've parked our caravans near your house, that doesn't mean to say that the motorway is going anywhere near here. And you're wrong when you say we decide where it's going to be. We only make our report. The rest is up to the County Council.'

'Yes, of course. I'm sorry. But this whole business has us worried.'

He nodded understandingly. 'These new roads always upset somebody—or nearly always. But very often it turns out for the best, you know. People never like being moved out of their old houses and into new ones, but sometimes they're glad afterwards. And in some instances the outlook is better with the old property down. A motorway can improve the terrain—look graceful.'

'Well, a motorway wouldn't improve this valley—which is our outlook,' Melanie said warmly. 'And our house may be old, but it's not ready for demolition yet by a long way.'

'Don't get me wrong,' Eric Eaton said swiftly. 'Unofficially, I'm on your side, naturally. But I wouldn't dare say that to just anyone. We simply daren't take sides. That's why they prefer strangers rather than local engineers and surveyors. Mind you, if I *had* any influence I'd bring it to bear for your sake. I really would.'

'Why?' Melanie asked suspiciously.

He grinned. 'Why? Because I like you, for one thing. For another, your house looks good and you've got a wonderful view here. I'd feel the same in your place. So I hope you're going to forget my job so that we can be friends.'

Melanie laughed and put down her cup. 'You've got quite a way with you, haven't you? Thanks for the coffee. I'm afraid I have to go now.'

He rose with her. 'Couldn't I persuade you to go out with me one evening? I'm really quite harmless.'

'I've only got your word for that,' she retorted.

He put his hand on his heart. 'My word of *honour*.'

'As a gentleman and all that?'

'As a gentleman and all that.'

'In that case—'

'You will? Good. What about tonight?' he asked promptly.

'Sorry, I have my music lesson tonight.'

'Music lesson?' he echoed. 'Are you learning to play the piano or something?'

'Not "something". The piano.'

'Couldn't you skip it?'

23

'Why should I when there's all the rest of the week to choose from? Besides, I wouldn't want to. I like it.'

'How far have you got? Are you past the five finger exercise stage yet?'

'I hope so.'

'What sort of stuff do you play—not highbrow and all that?'

'Yes, and I really must go. I'm a working girl.'

'Tomorrow evening at seven?' he suggested. 'We could have a meal somewhere.'

'Yes, all right. Thank you.'

'I'll call for you.'

She waved goodbye to him, and smiled to herself as she plunged back through the coppice. He really was quite nice, and she loved meeting new people.

'You've been a long time,' her mother said when she went back into the house. 'Did you find out anything?'

'Yes, he's a civil engineer. They're doing some surveying.' Melanie remembered what her father had said. But it was no use trying to hide the truth. Her mother would almost certainly find out sooner or later.

'Surveying? It isn't anything to do with the new motorway, is it?'

'Well—yes. But they're doing the whole area. They're only camping here for convenience.'

Mrs Lawrence, however, looked troubled. 'Oh dear, how awful! How dreadful if they decide to—to bring it up here.'

Melanie kissed her cheek. 'Don't worry about it, Mother. Try not to think about it. It may never happen.'

'But what if it does?'

'Well then, we'll—have a nice new house. I must go now. Mustn't have the shop without one of its owners for too long.'

Melanie hoped, as she drove back into town, that she had made light of the problem sufficiently to please her father. But this bogey of having to find somewhere else to live might have to be faced some time. Soon, Eric and whoever he would be working with would be tramping all along the hillside and down the valley with their surveying instruments. Her mother would see them from the window. It was going to be difficult not to talk about the matter.

And so it proved. When she arrived home that evening her mother was full of the two men she had seen taking measurements, setting up field surveying instruments and generally tramping around.

'One of them even came to the house to ask if we had an outside tap where they could get drinking water. I call that adding insult to injury.'

'Mother, they haven't done us any injury yet. Did you give them permission?'

'Well, how could I refuse? He had almost certainly seen the tap we use for watering the garden as he came past the side of the house. Besides, he seemed a pleasant enough young man.'

'Ah! Did he tell you his name?'

'Eric something or other.'

'Eric Eaton. He was the one I met this morning. I'm going out for a meal with him tomorrow evening.'

'Really? Good heavens, you young people don't waste any time, do you? But it might be a good thing.'

'How, Mother?'

'You might be able to influence him.'

'You mean about the motorway? Not a hope. They simply make their report. The rest is up to the Council —he told me.'

'Well, of course he would *have* to say that, wouldn't he? But I wouldn't be at all surprised if—'

Melanie shook her head. 'No, Mother, we mustn't. We can't expect any favours. We shall just have to wait and see, and if the worst happens—'

'What do you mean, if the worst happens? I don't

want to leave this house. It would upset me dreadfully. I couldn't stand the upheaval.'

'Oh yes, you could, Mother,' Melanie said quietly, but not without a twinge of conscience as she thought of what her father had said to her.

Helen Lawrence's lips quivered. 'You—you simply don't understand, Melanie. How could you?'

'But I do understand. I love this house and the valley just as much as you do, but it's no use closing our eyes to what might happen.'

'I—I refuse to listen to you. And if you won't try to influence that young man, then I will!'

She bustled out of the room, and Melanie looked after her with a sigh. If only her mother would try to face up to realities more readily. She began to wish she had not promised to see Eric either tomorrow or any other evening.

As she went upstairs to change the following evening, her mother asked in a too-casual voice:

'That young man calling for you?'

Melanie hesitated, then swiftly made a decision. 'No, Mother, I'm going along to his caravan. I—wasn't sure what time I'd be home.'

It wasn't quite a lie, even though Eric had said he would call for her. But she could not bear it if her mother started trying to influence him. The best thing would be to prevent his coming to the house if possible. She had noticed two cars parked on the grass verge near the gate leading to the meadow where the caravans were sited. One of them would undoubtedly be his. The other, she presumed, belonged to his boss.

At a quarter to seven she knocked on the door of his caravan. He might think it odd her changing their arrangement, but she would have to risk that. She could hear voices inside, however, as she stood waiting for the door to open, and wondered if she should go away again. She might be intruding on a work conference.

But the next moment the door opened. As she expected Eric looked faintly surprised.

'Hello, Melanie. Am I late?'

'No, I just thought I'd pop along as I was ready early. But if I'm interrupting anything I can go away again.'

'No need for that. Come on in and meet my boss. What we were talking about can wait until tomorrow.'

She stepped inside, and as she entered the main part of the caravan she came face to face with D. K. Hamilton.

CHAPTER II

Melanie was staggered. That this man had anything to do with the proposed new motorway was the last thing she had expected. They looked at each other for a moment, but it was impossible to tell whether he, in his turn, was surprised to see her or not.

'Melanie, this is Drew Hamilton, the civil engineer in charge of the survey,' Eric said. 'Drew, this is—'

'I know. We've met,' Drew Hamilton cut in sharply. He gave Melanie a cold stare, then with a brief nod he went out without another word. There was a short, rather uncomfortable silence. Melanie broke it.

'I'm sorry. Is he always like that?'

Eric sighed. 'I don't know. I mean—I can't make him out sometimes. But there's no need for *you* to apologise. Come on, let's go. I'm hungry, and I expect you are.'

Chilled by Drew Hamilton's cold stare and brusque manner, she couldn't help wondering what exactly had been going through his mind. Eric had hinted that he could be odd sometimes, but he had been talking amicably enough from what she could hear before she had arrived.

'Where did you and Drew meet, then?' Eric asked as they drove into town.

Melanie told him. 'But I had no idea what his job was, still less that he had anything to do with this motorway project. How long have you known him?'

'Oh—not long. Little over a week, actually. He's good at his job. I've never met one better—or even half as good. And he's fine to work with. It's just that he's —well, not exactly unfriendly, but he doesn't talk about himself very much. You know how it is with some people. Within a few days of knowing them and in a few sentences you know most of what there is to know about them—their background, whether they're married or single, and so on. The bloke you're working with either shows you a photograph of his family or his girl. But not this man.'

'So you—don't even know whether he's married or not?'

Eric shook his head. 'He acts like a man who has something he wants to forget.'

Melanie wondered what it was. An unhappy love affair? An unsuccessful marriage? But why had he given her such a cold look just now?

'I thought perhaps he disapproved of my coming to your caravan,' she ventured.

'Good heavens, why should he? It's no business of his who comes to my van. At any rate, not after working hours.' Then Eric grinned. 'Maybe he was jealous.'

'Jealous?'

'Yes. Perhaps he'd like an attractive woman to come calling on him.' But to Melanie Drew Hamilton had seemed more annoyed than jealous, though she couldn't see that he had any right to be either.

She and Eric spent a pleasant enough evening together. They had dinner at the Portland Hotel, and during the meal he told her something about his background, how his parents had struggled to send him to university and what he hoped to become.

'You're not married, I take it?' she asked.

He shook his head. 'In my college days I was working too hard to form any serious attachments. I felt I owed something to my parents.'

'And now?'

'The right girl just hasn't come along. Most of the time I live at home, and the money I give my mother helps a little to repay the folks for the sacrifices they made for me. Not all the fellows of my age think that way, I know, but—'

29

'I admire you for it,' Melanie told him.

'And what about you?' he asked. 'How is it that an attractive girl like you isn't at least engaged?'

She smiled. 'I could give the same answer as you. So far, the right man just hasn't come along.'

'Do you want to get married?'

'I suppose so. Doesn't everybody?'

'It's normal,' he conceded. 'But I think it's awfully easy to get married for the wrong reason.'

'What do you call the wrong reason?'

'Well—out of loneliness, to have a place of your own, or even for money; anyway, things like freedom at home, a bachelor flat or sharing one—none of these are quite the same as marriage.'

Melanie thought for a moment. 'I suppose the truth is, one should never marry for any reason. Only because you're so much in love that you can't live without each other.'

'It's the ideal, of course. The trouble is, often the most ill-suited people fall in love and afterwards regret it.'

'If they're all that ill-suited, do you really think they could have been genuinely in love in the first place?' she argued.

He grimaced. 'You've got a point. Maybe love means different things to different people.'

After this they began to talk of other things, and Melanie learned that though he did not care for classical music he did like plays.

'In that case, you must go to the Civic Theatre here in Chesterfield,' she told him.

'You'll come with me?'

'Why, yes—if I'm free on the night you want to go. You have to book well in advance, though.'

They lingered over their coffee, then strolled through the town for a little while before making their way back to where Eric parked his car. It was still not really late when they drove towards home, and Melanie would have loved to have invited him into the house to meet her parents, but the thought of what her mother might say to him restrained her. He parked the car in its usual place and insisted on walking the short distance to the house.

At the bottom of the short drive, however, lit by an old street lamp, she turned to say goodnight to him.

'Thanks for a very pleasant evening, Eric.'

'Not at all. It's I who should thank you. When can I see you again? Tomorrow? The next day?'

She smiled. 'Whoa, there! I'm afraid I'm fully occupied one way and another for the rest of the week.'

Again, she felt a twinge of conscience about him. Mid-week she was having some friends to supper and could have invited him, but—

'Then what about Sunday?'

She shook her head. 'I'm sorry—really. Weather permitting I'm—'

She broke off, wondering whether she would be wrong in telling him about her provisional date with his boss. But he took her up.

'Weather permitting you're—what—?'

'I'm—acting as guide to Drew Hamilton.'

'No! Now I *know* he was jealous!'

She felt her cheeks colouring in the soft lighting. 'Don't be silly. He asked me on impulse, and I'm sure he's regretted it already.'

'On impulse? I doubt if Drew Hamilton ever does anything on impulse. But what do you mean by "weather permitting"?'

'We said we wouldn't go if it rained.'

'Ah, then if it does? Come and have tea with me, then we can take a run out to some nice little country pub or club.'

'But that doesn't seem fair. Wouldn't you normally be going home?'

31

'Not necessarily. And this week-end my folks will be away.'

It was an odd circumstance, but she promised to do as he said if her engagement with Drew Hamilton was cancelled. She went indoors rather worriedly, but told herself that Eric would no doubt meet other people during the course of his job in the area.

But almost the first thing her mother said to her when Melanie joined her parents in the living room was: 'Why didn't you bring the young man in for a coffee?'

'I wanted to have an early night.'

'An early night?' her mother echoed. 'Why? What's wrong with you?'

Melanie sighed. It had been a lame excuse. No one in the Lawrence household ever went to bed early unless they were ill.

'Nothing's wrong with me, Mother. I just didn't want to bring Eric in, that's all.'

Her father looked up interestedly from the book he was reading.

'Why not, Melanie?' he asked.

Melanie did not want to answer. She simply shook her head and kept silent. But this wasn't good enough for her mother. Helen Lawrence gave her daughter a keen glance.

'I know. You were afraid I'd say something to him about this motorway business, weren't you?'

'Were you, Melanie?' Richard asked quietly.

Melanie heaved another sigh. 'Yes, I was,' she admitted.

'But why?' demanded Helen.

'Oh, Mother, can't you see? It would be embarrassing to both of us. I've told you, he's not open to influence. It wouldn't be right, anyway. There are other people who are concerned too, remember.'

'I'm—I'm not interested in other people. All I want is to save our house, and I'd have thought you would

32

want that, too. But of course you'll be getting married one of these days and having a house of your own somewhere else, so it hardly matters to you.'

'Mother!'

Richard Lawrence put down his book and went swiftly to his wife's side. 'Sweetheart, don't upset yourself or you won't sleep tonight.'

Melanie became aware of familiar feelings of guilt. Her mother was not really as selfish as she had sounded. She *was* interested in other people. It was just that this house meant so much to her. And it was true, she supposed, that if she herself married, she would live elsewhere.

'I'm sorry, Mother,' she found herself saying. 'I didn't mean to upset you, but it really would be much better for yourself if you could wait and see without worrying too much.'

'How can I?' came the half-tearful reply.

'But don't you see—'

'Melanie,' her father cut in, 'I think you'd best not say any more tonight.'

But the mild rebellion which had begun of late to make itself felt in Melanie was not to be so easily subdued. A kind of recklessness took possession of her. She rose to her feet feeling compelled to say one more thing.

'Mother, I'd like to have brought Eric in. I'd like to invite him in quite often. He's lonely and away from home. But if I do, I want it to be on a social level—for *his* sake, not just because we want to try to influence him. Where the motorway eventually runs has nothing to do with him. He and Drew Hamilton just simply have a job to do. They'll make their report, and that will be that. Now, may I invite him in occasionally while he's here without your trying to influence him?'

Her parents stared at her in astonishment. Wide-eyed, her mother's glance went swiftly to her husband and then back to Melanie.

'How can you talk to me like that? I don't know what's come over you lately, Melanie, really I don't.' She dabbed her eyes.

Richard looked at his daughter reproachfully but said nothing. Normally, Melanie would have let the matter drop, but now she metaphorically dug her heels in.

'You still haven't answered my question, Mother.'

Helen gave a despairing, helpless gesture. 'But of course you can invite the young man in any time. I'll try not to mention the motorway, but it will look much more unnatural than it would if it *were* mentioned. Surely you can see that?'

'It will, you know, Melanie,' interposed her father, resuming his seat as his wife appeared to be composing herself.

'Talk about it perhaps, yes. But that's a far different thing from trying to influence him—which would be pointless in any case.'

Helen sighed. 'All right, dear, I'll do my best,' she said in a tone one might use with a truculent child. 'I'd hate to feel the boy was lonely. And what about the other young man? Hamilton, did you say his name was? Why not ask them both in one evening?'

But at that Melanie shook her head. 'I don't know about that, Mother. He's different. He's the boss, and he's not exactly a young man.'

'Then your father can invite him, can't you, Richard?'

'Yes, of course, dear, if you wish.'

Melanie gave up. The situation was getting beyond her. How was it she had managed to get herself involved with both of these engineers? She felt she did not dare mention to either her mother or father that she had also arranged to go out with Drew. This would probably lead to an even more complicated discussion. She could only hope that it would rain on Sunday and their outing into Derbyshire's countryside would be put off. Then perhaps she could invite Eric to tea—and hope for the best.

But Sunday dawned fine. It was cool and there was a cutting east wind blowing, but it was fine, and after breakfast the sun came out. At about ten o'clock the telephone rang. Melanie flew to answer it before her mother did, and as she had anticipated it was Drew Hamilton.

'Shall I call for you in half an hour?' he asked.

'Er—yes, I'll be ready,' she answered.

It was going to be useless trying to prevent either of the two men from calling at the house, she decided. She was really beginning to wonder whether she had been wise to accept invitations from them at all. To other people who might also be affected by the proposed new motorway she was certainly exposing herself to the accusation of trying to bring influence to bear on them. Another thought suddenly occurred to her. Was that the reason why Drew Hamilton had been so annoyed when she called at Eric's caravan? It could be.

She was all ready to go and looking out for Drew from her bedroom window when his car pulled up outside the house. She ran down immediately thinking she would be in time to prevent his ringing the doorbell. That way, introductions could be put off and might not even take place at all. But her mother was already outside, meeting him. He had apparently introduced himself.

'Ah, good morning, Mr Hamilton. I was just coming out for a breath of fresh air. Lovely morning, isn't it?'

'Mr Hamilton, this is my mother,' Melanie said resignedly.

He put out his hand. 'Good morning, Mrs Lawrence. Yes, indeed, it *is* a lovely morning.'

Helen beamed, 'Won't you come in and have a cup of coffee before you go—and meet my husband?'

Drew Hamilton accepted gravely. 'Thank you, that would be very nice.'

35

Helen led the way indoors, Melanie and Drew following.

'We really mustn't delay too long, Mother. It might turn to rain,' Melanie said rather desperately.

'Well, if it does, dear, there's always another day, isn't there? In any case, I think you might bring Mr Hamilton back to lunch.'

'Mother, we're going out to lunch.'

'Are you? You didn't tell me.' She led the way into the very pleasant sitting room which she kept immaculate, continually having re-decorating done, replacing carpet and furniture whenever either grew in the least shabby. 'Melanie isn't usually so thoughtless,' she told him. 'I think it must be the spring. But do sit down and I'll go and put the coffee on to brew.'

Melanie suppressed a sigh and gave Drew an apologetic smile.

'I'm sorry. Mother does like meeting people.'

'Why apologise?' he returned. 'It's very pleasant, and extremely nice of her.' He glanced around. 'What a beautiful room this is. Lovely. Your mother has exquisite taste. Does she play the piano, too?' he queried as his glance fell on the concert grand at the far end of the rather large room. 'Or is that your accomplishment only?'

'Mother plays a little, but not very much. She sings. She has quite a good soprano voice, not strong, but very clear and sweet.'

'Sounds praise indeed. And what about your father?'

'He makes a fair crack at a tenor. I don't sing at all,' she told him before he could ask her. 'I concentrate on the piano.'

'Won't you play something for me now while we're waiting for coffee?'

Melanie rose, and without music began to play. First she played Beethoven's haunting *Für Elise*, then Chopin's 'Minute Waltz '—two short, relatively simple,

36

yet effective pieces. There was not the time this morning for longer works, and though she rarely felt nervous about playing in front of strangers, she did not feel she could trust herself to perform anything before Drew Hamilton which needed a great deal of concentration. She was far too aware of him.

As she played the downhill run of the Chopin waltz her mother entered, closely followed by her father.

'Don't stop, dear,' Helen murmured as Melanie swung around.

'That was quite beautiful,' Drew said in a surprised tone. 'You have a remarkably fine touch.'

Helen smiled and introduced the two men. 'Isn't it a shame, Richard? They're going out to lunch. See if you can get them to change their minds while I go and attend to the coffee.'

Richard sat down and Drew resumed his seat. Melanie stayed where she was on the piano stool. Would Drew allow himself to be persuaded?

'I suppose you've quite made up your minds about going out?' Richard asked.

'That was the invitation,' Drew answered. 'In return for Melanie acting as my guide. So it's really up to her.'

'If we leave it until after lunch we shan't have time to see anything,' Melanie pointed out.

'Well, the answer is simple. Come back and have supper with us, Drew. That will please my wife enormously.'

'Thank you,' Drew said. 'I'd like that.'

This was true Derbyshire hospitality, but Melanie had misgivings and wished her father had left it to her to invite Drew back. She couldn't help feeling that by the end of the day Drew might have had enough of the Lawrences. Of herself, at any rate. He was in a sufficiently good humour at present, but he seemed to be a man of varying moods. His brusqueness of the other evening was still fresh in her mind, and she did not believe for a moment that this was due to jealousy of Eric on her behalf.

Her mother was indeed delighted that Drew was coming back to supper.

'But don't be late,' she admonished. 'In fact if you could get home about seven we could have a little music before supper. I'm sure Drew would like to hear you play again, Melanie.'

'Yes, indeed,' murmured Drew.

With extreme difficulty they managed to get away by eleven-thirty, and already the mouth-watering smell of the Sunday joint was drifting from the kitchen. Drew sniffed appreciatively and Helen seized on it immediately.

'You might just as well stay to lunch. It won't be long now.'

'Mother, if we do—'

Drew came to her rescue. 'If we do, I shall very likely nod off afterwards, then it will be tea time— Thanks all the same, Mrs Lawrence. Besides, I've booked a table at a hotel.'

At last they were away. 'Did you want to stay home?' Melanie asked with a twinge of conscience.

He laughed. 'It was tempting. Such a homely atmosphere. Is your mother always like that?'

'She can be very persuasive.' Melanie felt she was putting it mildly. She loved her mother, but through the years Melanie had learned that one needed to have a will of one's own to stand up to her mother's gentle, thrusting way of getting people to do what she wanted.

Drew flicked her a swift glance. 'I meant—warm-hearted, motherly—even to strangers.'

'She's always warm-hearted,' returned Melanie. 'And motherly, too, though not necessarily always to strangers.'

'Then I'm honoured.'

Melanie made no further comment. Her mother *was* warm-hearted. She was hospitable, and with people she liked she could be charming. She had very probably taken a genuine liking to Drew. But had she also been thinking that by offering hospitality to him she would be able to influence him to their advantage with regard to the motorway?

'I suppose your own mother is pretty much the same?' she ventured, still anxious in case she had done her mother less than justice, and afraid also of being misunderstood.

He took so long in answering she wondered if indeed he was condemning her. Then he answered flatly:

'I never knew my mother.'

'Oh,' she said, slightly taken aback. 'Oh, I'm sorry.'

'No need to be sorry,' he said brusquely. 'What you've never had you don't miss.'

Melanie did not altogether agree with this familiar statement, but thought it best not to pursue the subject. While she felt sure he had been conscious of the outgoing warmth of her mother, a man like Drew Hamilton, his own master and having authority over others, would not take kindly to any suggestion of pity, no matter how slight or well meant.

'Where did you book a table for lunch?' she asked him.

'At Monsal Head.'

'That was very clever of you.'

She flicked him a sidelong glance and saw his lips curve into a humorous smile.

'Yes, wasn't it? As a matter of fact I made a few enquiries at one of the locals, and they recommended it. They also said that booking was essential at this time of year on account of it being out of season.'

'It's fairly essential almost at any time because of the hotel's remoteness. Except for the glorious view you get of the Dale from there, no hotel could hope to do much business, but you get a good meal and it's nicer than going into Bakewell. There are too many traffic jams there these days.'

Without any prompting from her he took the road to Baslow and the scene became gradually more wild as the road cut through open moorland, twisted around purple hills, or climbed steeply to plunge down into valleys again.

'You don't need a guide,' Melanie chaffed.

'I most certainly do,' he asserted. 'Besides, it gets awfully boring sitting in a car for mile after mile on one's own.'

'I see. So it wasn't my company in particular you wanted. Just anyone would have done equally well.'

'No, not just anyone.'

He was only being polite, of course. But Melanie gave a smile which no doubt could have been called a self-satisfied one and settled down in her seat even more comfortably.

'Of course you can't hope to see the entire Peak District in one day—and a very short one at that,' she said.

'I'm not expecting to. I thought we'd have lunch first, then take in either Haddon Hall or Chatsworth on the way back. Just take a look at the gardens. The houses won't be open until later in the spring, will they?'

'Easter.' If he was interested in historic and famous houses, Melanie couldn't help wondering why he had suggested a tour today. But of course the Derbyshire moors and its hills and dales were beautiful at all times of the year.

'Fascinating countryside,' commented Drew, almost as if reading her thoughts. 'So wild—'

'But in the Dales so picturesque. How long are you expecting to be in this area, Mr Hamilton?'

'A few weeks—a month maybe. There's quite a lot to do. But why the formality all at once? Do you want me to call you Miss Lawrence?'

'No, of course not. I'm sorry.'

40

There was a short silence. Then Drew said: ' By the way, I had no idea you knew my assistant.'

' I didn't—until very recently. In fact I didn't meet him until after you and I sat at lunch together. I—was curious when the two caravans appeared in the field, and as I often go there when I want to take a walk, I went along to investigate, as it were, and came across him.'

' It didn't take you long to get acquainted.'

' I suppose not.'

Drew said, after a pause, ' He's a very likeable young man, don't you think?'

' Yes, I do.' She took a sly glance at his profile. ' I —er—got the impression the other evening that you disapproved—either of my friendship with Eric or of my calling at his caravan.'

' It isn't any business of mine to approve or disapprove,' he answered distantly. ' If I appeared to make my departure quickly, it was because I had work to do.'

Melanie felt strangely abashed by his answer, and could have kicked herself for trying to probe into his thoughts and feelings. Clearly he was not a man with whom one could assume any familiarity. He was one whom it would be very difficult to know intimately.

A silence fell between them, but fortunately they soon arrived at Baslow, that charming village set in a valley of luxuriant meadows with wooded hills and rocks climbing up to rolling moorland, and where a lovely three-arched bridge crossed the river Derwent. The sun came out and they left the car to stroll beside the river and to look at the ancient humped bridge where there was the quaint little stone toll-house said to be the smallest in England. They also visited the church situated between the two bridges and Melanie showed Drew the ancient dog-whip near the door.

' What on earth was that for?' he asked.

' To drive dogs out of the church if they went in in

search of their masters. Some say it was also used to wake up the congregation if they snored!'

He laughed. 'How extraordinary. To hang on to such a relic, I mean. And to think the British have a world-wide reputation for being fanatical animal-lovers. But then people had fewer finer feelings in those days, either towards animals or each other.'

'Maybe.' They walked back to the car. 'Eyam is not far from here,' Melanie told him.

'Eyam?' he queried. 'The name rings a bell.'

'The plague village. I'm sure you remember. A box of old clothes was sent from London in the time of the plague to a tailor. The journeyman who opened the box caught the plague and died within four days. It spread rapidly. In a year and a month three hundred and fifty people had died. A lot for a small village. Many of the village people were preparing to leave the place, but rather than spread the plague still wider the Rector persuaded them to stay and isolate themselves. They arranged for food to be brought from outside and left at certain places like distant rocks to be collected at stated times. A tragic story for such a lovely morning, but there's courage and heroism in it too.'

Drew nodded. 'You know the story very well.'

'There's more, really. The rector's wife played her part in helping to allay the panic and the fears of the womenfolk. She worked alongside her husband, and in the end she became a victim, too. But I won't depress you with any more. I only told you at length to show that people with what you called "finer feelings" did exist in those far-off days.'

He opened the car door for her. 'You've proved your point. A tale of heroism and courage will always bear the telling even on a morning such as this.'

At Monsal Head Drew stood and looked down at the Dale speechless with wonder. Far below, the river wound its way through a pasture in which cattle grazed and ran under a charmingly picturesque little bridge to disappear between two great folds of hills.

'This is almost more beautiful than the Lakes,' he murmured. 'And that's saying something.'

'I knew you'd like it.'

'I was told by my informant at the local that it was "very nice". That surely must be the understatement of the year. Do you feel like making the descent? We might not be able to after a good lunch.'

She agreed, and they made their way down by a series of twisting narrow paths and steps cut in the earth, or sometimes made by the roots of trees. Once Drew took her hand to guide her over a rough spot and she found his touch strong and cool. They stood on the tiny bridge and looked down into the rapidly running water, then meandered along the bank of the river, pausing every now and then to gaze down into the clear water and watch the fish darting to and fro like flashes of silver.

The day took on a strange enchantment. Melanie had never felt quite this way before—this feeling of magic, of timelessness. Neither spoke a great deal, but after a while Drew glanced at his watch.

'We'd better go on up and have our lunch.'

'Yes.'

They retraced their steps. 'This is certainly a wonderful place,' Drew said slowly.

Melanie glanced at his uplifted profile. It was not possible that he could be feeling quite the same way as herself.

'Nature has a strange effect at times,' she said, almost speaking her thoughts aloud. 'These timeless hills, the beauty of the valley—'

'And the spring.'

'Yes, the spring.'

Drew had ordered a delicious lunch—turtle soup followed by roast duckling served with sauces, feather-light croquette potatoes and button sprouts, and to drink, a cool, sparkling white wine called Golden Guinea.

' What did you and Eric do the other evening?' Drew asked with a suddenness which startled her.

' We—had dinner at the Portland.'

' And what did you do after that?'

She looked at him in mild surprise mingled with amusement. ' We took a stroll around the town.'

' And very nice, too, I'm sure,' he said with a touch of irony.

Her humour faded. ' You *do* disapprove, don't you?'

' No, not exactly. It's just that—when we're on an assignment of this nature, surveying for a proposed motorway which might result in houses being affected, we don't usually become too—personally involved, shall we say, with any of the people who might be concerned.'

Her eyes widened at this. ' But you yourself—'

' I know. But I asked you to come on this excursion with me before I knew where you lived.'

' And now you're regretting it?'

' I didn't say that.'

' When did you find out that I lived at Hillrise?' she asked him.

' The day after you called at Eric's caravan.'

' So you really could have sent me a note putting the outing off?'

' Precisely.'

' Then why didn't you?' she demanded in exasperation.

Unexpectedly, he smiled. ' Because I didn't want to.'

It was as difficult to know whether she could take this as a compliment or not. Melanie certainly concluded that this would be the last time, as well as the first, that he would ask her to come either on a tour of the Derbyshire countryside or anything else.

But he went on: ' Why should I pass up an opportunity to spend the day in the company of a charming girl like you?'

Melanie could scarcely contain her astonishment. She had not thought him the kind of man to make pretty speeches. Was he, at heart, a Casanova? A sort of wolf in sheep's clothing?

'Why do you look so surprised?' he asked disconcertingly.

'Well, I—I *am* surprised.'

'Really? Why? Did you think me incapable of paying a compliment?'

'Not—incapable exactly.'

He eyed her with some amusement. 'Have another glass of wine. You should never judge an apple by its skin.'

'Obviously not.'

It was a noncommittal reply, and Melanie felt she had unwittingly scored, as it had the effect of silencing him for a minute or two. At any rate, he concentrated on his apple pie and cream. She was finding him, increasingly, an interesting and an intriguing companion. He was certainly a much more complex character than Eric. Eric was a 'nice boy', frank, pleasant to be with, easy to know, uncomplicated. This man, sitting at the other side of the table, was difficult to fathom, exasperating, and exciting, as complex as a modern computer.

'Well?' queried Drew as he paid the bill after the meal. 'Where next? I'm in your hands.'

'Are you?' she parried, giving him a wry glance.

His lips twitched with amusement. 'What a disbeliever you are! No one could put anything across you, could they?'

'It has been known. But of course, once one has bitten into that apple you were talking about, at least one knows whether it's sweet or sour, hard or soft.'

He grinned, obviously enjoying her repartee. 'And what conclusions have you come to about me?'

'Very few as yet. But it's my guess that you didn't set out this morning without a thorough good look at a

45

map of this area. You'd be the very last person to rely completely on someone else.'

'Not bad,' he conceded. 'All the same I'll leave the navigating to you. And I shall expect to be told something about Chatsworth and Haddon Hall. It's part of the contract.'

'Oh, is it?'

'Yes. You should read the small print.'

From Monsal Head Melanie directed him towards Bakewell—a place of long traffic queues in the height of summer, but a charming if sedate little town and of quite some agricultural importance.

'This is where the famous Bakewell tarts originated, I suppose?' Drew said as they drove through its now quiet streets.

Melanie laughed. 'So they say. Actually, the name has nothing to do with cooking. In the Doomsday Book it's recorded as *Badequella*, which means Bath-well. But there were only ever two wells, and the town was never developed as a spa as Buxton was.'

'Very interesting. I knew you'd be a mine of information,' Drew said.

'Is that intended as sarcasm?'

'Of course not. Lots of people who visit these places —even the residents, sometimes—though they love the country and the place they live in—know very little about its history.'

'Well—' she conceded, 'I suppose I'm not a bookseller's daughter for nothing.'

He laughed shortly. 'A good many people who sell books don't know much about them, either. And I *don't* mean anyone in *your* shop,' he added swiftly.

Complimentary or merely honesty? Melanie wondered. But whichever it was it was pleasant.

They didn't stop to explore Bakewell, but followed the road leading to Haddon Hall, one of the most attractive of England's ancient manor houses.

'How old is it?' Drew asked as they passed through the gateway in the great tower into the courtyard.

'It was built mostly about six hundred years ago by Sir George Vernon.'

'Ah! The father of the famous Dorothy.'

'That's right. A very romantic tale, hers.'

'What happened?'

'She eloped, of course, with the handsome Sir John Manners.'

'You sound rather cynical,' he observed.

'I'm not, in the least. In similar circumstances I would have done the same.'

'You would?' He gave her a speculative look as if trying to assess her true character. 'I believe you would, too. You'd defy anyone if you wanted a thing badly enough.'

'That makes me sound ruthless!'

'Well, let me put it another way. You can be— fearless, courageous, defiant even, if a thing is important to you or you felt it was right.'

Melanie laughed. 'Thank you for that character reading,' she said, feeling an extraordinary pleasure at his conclusions.

They strolled along the beautiful terraced gardens laid out for the most part as long ago as the seventeenth century. Across the river, winding through the meadows below, Melanie pointed out the old packhorse bridge over which Dorothy Vernon was said to have escaped to her lover.

But Melanie's favourite house was Chatsworth, built on a rising slope above the river Derwent. It stood in a deer park ten miles around, with hill and woods, gardens and lawns, cascades and terraces; and on the south front a beautiful lake making a glorious vista.

Drew was absolutely charmed. 'Built by?' he queried.

'The fourth Earl of Devonshire, later Duke.'

'Lucky man—to be able to create something like that for his wife.'

So far as Melanie knew the Earl had neither built the house nor created the gardens for his wife, and she wondered why Drew had assumed so.

'Is that what you would like to do—create a place like this for the woman you marry?' she queried.

His shoulders lifted. 'Wouldn't any man?'

Melanie doubted it, but she did not argue with him. She felt only a twinge of envy for the woman lucky enough to be loved by him and to marry him.

CHAPTER III

At home a Sunday high tea was more usual, but today Helen Lawrence had prepared what was for them an almost elaborate supper. Melanie guessed that her mother had been busy the whole of the afternoon. She had made a delicious soup—in which she specialised—had baked a chicken and ham pie with absolute melt-in-the-mouth crust and all kinds of delectable flavours, also a sweet for dessert so elaborately decorated it must have taken simply ages to do.

Melanie said nothing, however, and her mother's labours were rewarded by Drew's obvious enjoyment of the meal as well as his compliments afterwards.

' If you had sons, Mrs Lawrence,' he said, ' they'd be absolutely spoilt.'

Melanie saw her mother's expression change. Unwittingly, Drew had said the wrong thing, and she hoped he wouldn't guess that he had done so and labour the point by apologising or covering up.

But he went on: ' As it is, I expect your husband is spoilt with your good cooking—not to mention your daughter.'

' I doubt if they always appreciate it, Mr Hamilton,' Helen said mildly.

' I'm sure they *do*—and please call me Drew.'

Richard and Melanie affirmed this statement naturally, but Helen was scarcely listening. Her eyes had taken on a wistful look.

' We did have a son. Has Melanie told you?' she said to him, greatly to Melanie's surprise. Her mother usually did not talk about Rory so easily. It was still too painful, even after all these years.

' Yes. The " Lawrence & Son "?'

Helen nodded, and Melanie saw her mother's eyes

brighten with threatened tears.

' I expect Melanie has been both son and daughter to you,' Drew went on in a matter-of-fact tone.

Helen's head came up sharply. Then she said slowly, as if making a discovery:

' Yes, I suppose she has.'

' And from all I hear, she's very talented too. As both of you are,' he added tactfully.

Richard laughed. ' I don't know about us. We sing a bit, Helen and I, but Melanie has the greater gift. Do you enjoy music, Drew?'

He nodded. ' I'm hoping to hear her play some more before I go.'

To Melanie's relief the motorway was not even mentioned. After supper she played the piano, then her parents sang a little. Apart from the occasional ' I like that', or ' What is that called?' Drew listened in silence. It was only when she was seeing him off that he remarked:

' You play well.'

' Thank you.'

He gave her a direct look. ' Did you ever think of taking it up professionally?'

' I thought about it at one time, yes. But helping Father with the business seemed more important.'

' At one time—to use your own words—perhaps. But not now, surely?'

She smiled. ' I play at various charity concerts—and for the pleasure of my parents and friends. And of course it's a pleasure for me, too. If it were my profession it might cease to be a pleasure. It would be work, wouldn't it?'

' I suppose so. But wouldn't you like to have more time in which to play—and perhaps practise new works?'

Melanie was glad that they were not standing in full light. He had hit on a painful truth. She did often wish she had more time—time in which to practise more difficult works, to perfect her technique in general. She always tried to suppress such thoughts, but she could do nothing about the sudden strong desire to play which would come to her while she was attending to a customer or doing some other work in the shop. To have a piano always within reach, to be able to obey the impulse to play at any hour. This was her idea of heaven.

'One always needs more time, even if one has all the time in the world,' she said evasively.

He nodded. 'True. Well, goodnight—and thanks for being a most charming and interesting guide.'

She said goodnight and he strode off before she had scarcely got the words out of her mouth. No mention of seeing her again, even casually, no suggestion of a repeat outing. She sighed and went indoors. He was certainly the most unusual and unpredictable man she had ever encountered.

Naturally enough her mother and father were already talking about him, both having taken an immediate liking to him.

'And when are you seeing him again, darling?' asked Helen.

'I don't know, Mother. He didn't ask me.'

'Didn't ask you? But how extraordinary!'

Melanie laughed shortly. 'He's not an *ordinary* man.'

Her mother looked at her. 'No, I don't think he is,' she said slowly, 'but you'd like to see him again?'

Melanie collected her music together. 'I found him a very interesting person to be with, Mother, but whether I see him again or not is a matter of complete indifference to me.'

She saw the glance which passed between her mother and father, but pretended she had not, and after another few minutes went upstairs to her room. Without switching on the light she sat at the window and looked out. In the darkness she could see the lights from the two caravans, and down the valley those of the houses, twinkling through the trees like jewels, then beyond on the opposite hill to the glow that was the town.

Did she want Drew Hamilton to ask her out again? She smiled to herself and honestly acknowledged that it would be nice. Then her smile faded as she remembered what he had said about the surveyors not making friends with the people concerned in proposed new motorways. Perhaps he would even advise Eric not to see her again.

She moved away from the window and switched on the light. Life went on perfectly smoothly for what seemed ages, then one day someone new came into it and—

She pulled herself up. She was dramatising. One met new people quite frequently. What was so special about either of these two men? But she knew in her heart that, though Eric might be a nice, ordinary person, there was something very different about Drew Hamilton.

It was several days later that she saw Eric. He sought her out in the office at the shop.

' Sorry I haven't contacted you before now,' he said. ' I've been tied up.'

' You don't have to apologise,' she answered, asking him to sit down.

' I wasn't, really. I'm sorry for my own sake. How'd you get on with my boss the other day?'

Her shoulders lifted in assumed indifference. ' We had an interesting day. Lunch at Monsal Head, then a look at Haddon Hall and Chatsworth. From the outside, of course.'

' I sometimes think those places are more interesting from the outside than the inside,' he commented.

' That depends on whether you like antique furniture, works of art and so on.'

' Are you—er—seeing Drew again?' he queried.

' Why do you want to know?'

' Sorry, I shouldn't have asked. The point is: Am *I* going to see you again?'

'If you want to—and if you're sure your boss wouldn't object.'

'I don't care whether he does or not.'

'Brave man!'

Eric grinned. 'Oh, he's not so bad, really. What he needs is a woman who can match up to him.'

'Perhaps he's got one.'

'And perhaps he hasn't. Have dinner with me to-night. I'm fed up with eating out of tins.'

'That's not very flattering—if it's the only reason you want to see me again.'

'You know perfectly well it isn't. Anyway, I'll call for you around seven. Meanwhile, don't make any arrangements about Sunday without consulting me.'

He was only joking, of course, but Melanie thought it most unlikely that Drew Hamilton would repeat his invitation.

Eric drove them into Sheffield for a meal where the choice of places to eat were more numerous. Melanie relaxed in his company, and would not have mentioned Drew's name if he had not done so. Oddly enough he asked the same—or a similar—question as the one Drew had asked her.

'What did you and Drew do when you came back from seeing Haddon Hall and Chatsworth?'

Melanie couldn't help smiling, and she saw no reason to hide anything.

'He came back to our house for supper.'

Eric's eyes opened wide. 'Really?'

She nodded. 'He called for me in the morning, and my mother invited him back. She wanted us to have lunch at home, but if we had, we'd never have got away.' She glanced at Eric's face again. 'You look surprised.'

'I am—very. This is most unlike Drew. Normally, he tries to avoid becoming involved with any of the people who might be affected by a new motorway.'

'I know. He told me.'

' Mind you, there isn't always a beautiful girl in the picture.'

' Flattery will get you nowhere!'

' I'm not flattering you. But it only goes to prove—'

' What?'

' That he's just as susceptible as any other man.'

' Did you think he wasn't?'

' No-o, but—'

' But what?'

He shrugged. ' Nothing, really. It's just that— granted you're a very attractive woman, it's—odd some- how.'

Melanie was silent for a minute or two. There was something not quite right to her, too, but she was not sure what. It was from her mother she had inherited her good looks, but the idea that Drew had only asked her out because of the shape of her nose or her blonde hair was one which did not appeal to her at all. It was a fair enough reason, really, she supposed, and yet—

' What's on your mind?' came Eric's voice, breaking off her train of thought.

' Nothing, except that I probably won't be seeing him again. When he asked me to go with him into the country he had no idea who I was, where I lived or that I had any connection with the proposed new motorway.'

Eric's face lightened. ' Oh, I see.' Then he frowned again. ' All the same, he knew well enough when he accepted your mother's invitation to supper, didn't he?'

' I don't see that it's so terribly important,' Melanie said. ' After all, you and I are seeing each other, aren't we?'

' True.'

' And he hasn't said you can't?'

' His authority doesn't extend that far, and there's no law about it. It's just usually the accepted thing that we don't—fraternise. That was the word they used during World War Two regarding friendships between people in occupied countries and the enemy,' he added.

'It's not quite the same, though, is it? Fraternisation on our part—my parents and myself, that is—might be to our advantage. But if, as you say, the civil engineers have no influence as to where the motorway eventually goes, why all the fuss?'

'Ah, but not everybody *knows* that. You see?'

'So where does that leave us?' Melanie queried.

Eric grinned. 'It leaves me wanting to see you just as often as you will. As to Drew—well, it will suit me well enough if he stays right out of the picture.'

'Selfish philosophy,' Melanie said lightly.

'That's right.'

Eric cheerfully tackled his steak, while Melanie became lost again in her own thoughts. Did she want Drew to 'stay right out of the picture'? She gave a mental shrug. Life was like that—contrary. The thing one wanted most always just out of reach—like the proverbial biggest and best apple. Right at the top of the tree. The most luscious blackberries where one could not stretch without falling headlong into the centre of the bramble.

She attempted to marshal her thoughts, and reminded herself that the inaccessible was often a disappointment when one did manage to get it. Like the other man's grass being always greener. But why was she thinking this way at all? Drew Hamilton hardly came under the heading of the 'desirable, but inaccessible.' At least, not for her. True, she had found him interesting, but—

'A penny for them,' Eric said.

She shook her head. 'They're not worth it. Tell me —what sort of things do you do when you're on holiday?'

Eric embarked on an enthusiastic account of a holiday he had spent in Cornwall, mainly surf-riding, and Melanie was glad to have the conversation away from Drew.

She did not see Drew for several weeks. The surveying for the motorway was now taking them elsewhere than in the area of Hillrise, and Eric, whom she now saw regularly, told her that Drew had been going home for his week-ends.

'Got someone special up in the Lake District, I shouldn't wonder,' he added.

Melanie made no comment, but she was aware of a vague sense of disappointment.

But one day her father surprised her by saying casually: 'By the way, will you be in tonight? I've asked Drew Hamilton round to dinner.'

'You— But, Father, why?'

'Why not?'

Melanie scarcely knew what to answer. She was too taken by surprise and also very bewildered.

'But I thought—' she began, and then stopped.

Her father gave her a look of mild enquiry. 'Yes, my dear, what did you think?'

'Nothing.'

He smiled. 'Don't imagine that I'm going to talk about the motorway to him, because I'm not.'

'Then why?' she asked again.

'Because I like him. Besides, he asked me out to lunch one day. Didn't I tell you?'

'No, Father, you didn't.'

'Then I must have forgotten. So you see, quite apart from anything else, I owe him hospitality. You will be home?'

'I shall, but I was going to wash my hair.'

'Well, you can wash it another night, can't you? In any case, it looks all right to me. It always does.'

But Melanie thought it odd, Drew inviting her father to lunch and then accepting an invitation to dinner, in view of what he had said about not becoming personally involved with people who might be affected by proposed new motorways. She remembered every word of their conversation on the day they had gone into the country,

56

in particular his compliment about not passing up an opportunity to spend the day in 'the company of a pretty girl like you'. He could have asked her out again. Why hadn't he? The obvious answer was that he did not like her. Or was he being loyal to someone else? That special someone who lived near his home in the Lake District?

Melanie wished she were going out, and almost regretted having been brought up to be so truthful. She could easily have said that she was going out, and then done so. But why bother? she asked herself. It did not really matter one way or the other.

She arrived that evening to find her mother in a flurry of preparation. Much more than usually so when having anyone to dinner.

'Mother, why all this fuss? He isn't all that special.'

'No, dear? I thought he was.'

'To whom, Mother?'

'Well—to you, I thought. I certainly think he is,' Helen said blandly. 'Now go and get changed, dear, otherwise you won't be ready.'

Melanie gave up and went to her room. She would change only to please her mother. She had a bath, then hunted through her wardrobe for something that would not look as though she had dressed up specially for him. Unfortunately, she had very little that was really old, except for a pair of faded trousers she used for occasional gardening. She had recently given quite a large parcel of dresses and other items to a jumble sale, and she never wore anything which did not suit her. She reached for a trouser suit. She wouldn't be surprised if he disapproved. There were still some men about who disapproved of women in trousers, though they had been in fashion for some time. Her parents had raised their eyebrows the first time she had worn this particular suit. Perhaps Drew Hamilton would, too. The trousers were gold with rows of pleats on the lower edge of each leg, and the tunic a gay splash of red and gold with wide flowing sleeves. Her mother wanted her to change. Very well, she would.

She was fastening the tie belt when she heard Drew arrive. His deep voice and that of her father drifted up from the hall, then became muffled as they went, she supposed, into the sitting room. She looked at herself in the long mirror and couldn't help smiling. The trouser suit did something for her, gave her a certain air, and with her straight blonde hair—which did not, in actual fact, need washing—brushed back and fastened with a large hair ornament, she decided she liked her appearance, even if no one else would.

She did not hurry down. She tidied her room, put on a pair of red sandals, then went down into the kitchen.

'Do you want any help, Mother?'

'No, thank you, dear. We're just waiting for you, then we'll have a glass of sherry.'

'You shouldn't have waited. If I'd known—'

'That's all right, dear. But we'll go in now.' Helen swung round and her eyes shot wide open as she took in Melanie's appearance.

Melanie gave a mischievous smile. 'Like it?'

'Well, I—' gasped Helen, then she stopped. 'As a matter of fact, I do. I wasn't sure when you first tried it on, but now I think it looks—well—dashing.'

They went into the sitting room, and Melanie waited for both her father's and Drew's reaction. Her father's was immediate.

'Wow! Melanie, you look simply splendid,' he said.

Melanie was beginning to wish she had chosen to wear something quieter. The last thing she had wanted was to give Drew the impression of having dressed up specially for him.

'I didn't think you liked it, Father,' she answered.

'When did I say that? I think it's terrific, don't you, Drew?'

Drew had hidden his feelings much more successfully.
'I do indeed,' he said slowly.

They all sat down while Richard poured out drinks.
Drew continued to look at Melanie's suit.

'You have quite a flair for dress,' he said. 'I've
noticed before. Your father must pay you a very good
salary.'

He was hinting that she spent more money than she
should on clothes, of course, Melanie thought. But before
she could say anything her mother intervened.

'Oh, Melanie makes her own clothes—and designs
them.'

This did succeed in surprising Drew. 'Really? She's
full of surprises. What a wonderful wife she'll make
some fortunate man.'

Melanie knew a swift feeling of annoyance. What a
ridiculous thing to say, and she hated being talked at in
this way.

'My father pays me the same salary that he would
anyone else doing a responsible job,' she told him stiffly.
'I insist upon it. And I don't make my own clothes
for reasons of economy, but because I like doing it.'

'Melanie!' reproved her mother in a shocked tone.

But Drew's lips curved into a faint smile. 'You have
a very charming and talented daughter, Mrs Lawrence.'

Melanie drew an angry breath. 'Will you please stop
talking as if I weren't here—or were a three-year-old!'

'I'm sorry,' Drew said at once. 'I'm being very rude.
Forgive me.'

His apology made her feel worse than ever. Why did
she behave so unnaturally in this man's company? Then
she said something which appalled even herself.

'How's your work regarding the motorway progressing, Drew?'

Too late, she saw the swift look of surprise which
passed between her parents. She had said absolutely
the first thing which came into her head.

But Drew showed no reaction whatever. 'Oh, it's progressing—in the usual way. I should think we have about another month's work in the area.'

'Is that all?'

'Why? Did you imagine we'd be longer?'

'I—don't know. I hadn't thought about it.'

'And where will you be going when you've finished here?' Richard asked him.

'I'm not sure. Actually, I might take a holiday.'

Helen rose. 'That's always a good idea. Shall we go in to dinner now?'

One of the best views of the valley was from the dining room window, and the table was placed in the bay, guests being always seated to face the view. It was really inevitable that Drew should remark upon it, though Melanie was surprised that he did so, knowing as he surely must, where his remark might lead. But it was as though Melanie's question about the motorway had opened the door to a forbidden subject.

Helen sighed. 'Yes, it is lovely. That's why we bought this house. Melanie was born here. Have you any idea yet where your motorway will run?'

He shook his head. 'I can't tell you, Mrs Lawrence. And it isn't *my* motorway.'

Melanie noticed that he hadn't really answered her mother's question, and a horrible suspicion was forming in her mind.

'I suppose you've written a letter to the Council objecting should the motorway affect your house?' Drew asked her father.

'Yes, and I've received the usual reply.'

'Then that's all you can do, I'm afraid. I like a good view, too,' he went on, clearly turning the conversation into more general lines. 'In fact, I saw a piece of building land the other day with a superb view. I'm tempted to buy it, build myself a house.'

Melanie was glad that her mother—always swift in her

reactions—answered Drew.

'Really?' Helen said in astonishment. 'Where? You mean in Derbyshire?'

He nodded. 'Near Curbar. It's a lovely spot. I'd like you all to see it. Maybe you'll come over one day and we'll have lunch somewhere.'

'Lovely,' enthused Helen. 'We shall enjoy that, shan't we, Richard?'

Richard nodded. 'Of course.'

'Melanie?' queried Drew.

Melanie's eyes opened wide. 'I'm included, am I?'

'Certainly.'

She fumed inwardly. He was like someone offering them all a treat!

'If I'm free I'll come,' she answered stiffly.

'We must make sure you are,' he said. 'Let's make the date now. You tell me what weekends you're free and perhaps we can all fit in.'

'I'm afraid it really boils down either to Sundays or Wednesday half-day closing as far as Melanie and I are concerned,' Richard Lawrence said. 'And Wednesdays would be no use to you, would they?'

'It *is* one of my working days normally, yes, but I can take the odd half day off if it's convenient to the job. After all, I often work extra hours without extra pay.'

'You're salaried, of course.'

'That's right. So it can be Wednesday afternoon or Sunday. Evenings are impossible until there's more daylight.' Drew got out his pocket diary.

'We haven't anything fixed for either Wednesdays or Sundays for the next few weeks, have we, Richard?' Helen said readily.

'No, I don't think we have, dear.'

Only half listening to what was being said, Melanie found herself agreeing to keep free the following Wednesday afternoon. There were two things on her mind. The first was: Why was he building a house? To get married? And the other: Why was he being so friendly with her parents? Was it because he felt it was safe—that he already knew where the motorway was going to run so that 'fraternization' did not matter? He couldn't be accused of favouritism by anyone when it became known, for the simple reason that the motorway was going to run straight through their house. Either through it or so near it that they would simply have to move. It was the only possible explanation. As to the reason for his buying a plot of land and building a house, she could not understand why her mother had not asked him the question. But aggravatingly, she did not. Possibly because she had jumped to the same conclusion that anyone would. He was building a house because he was getting married. It was as simple as that. There was really no need to ask.

Melanie was quite glad when the evening was over. Most of the time Drew talked to her father. When she played the piano as requested, she knew she played badly, and as the evening wore on she felt more and more overdressed, a sensation which was new to her. Far from enjoying Drew's company and finding it stimulating as she had previously she was edgy, unsure of herself and felt entirely redundant, except perhaps to supply a little music. These kind of sensations were also new to her.

When he rose to go, it was her parents who saw him to the door, while Melanie busied herself tidying the music and plumping up cushions.

'Well,' her father said rubbing his hands together as he and Helen came back into the sitting room, 'that's what I call a very pleasant evening.'

'Yes, dear. You must invite him again—unless we leave that to Melanie.'

'I don't want you to leave anything of the sort to me,' Melanie answered swiftly.

'No, dear?'

' No, Mother.'

' Very well, dear,' Helen said, in her special pacifying tone, from which Melanie knew from experience that her mother was paying no attention whatever to what the other person had said.

Richard gave an indulgent smile in his wife's direction, then glanced at Melanie expectantly. But Melanie felt it would be useless to say anything further.

Following on this evening Drew took to popping in for a chat with her father quite frequently, a fact which Melanie found most disconcerting. Had he been a shy young man—of which there were still one or two about—she might have been justified in thinking—romantically, perhaps—that he was only making a pretence of coming to see her father in order to see herself. But Drew Hamilton was certainly not shy. It was not only disconcerting, it was most unflattering.

Eric had noticed his boss's visits to the house, too, and commented on them the next time Melanie went out with him for an evening. He came straight to the point.

' Drew is a frequent visitor to Hillrise these days,' he said. ' I wonder you have time for me.'

Melanie laughed shortly. ' It's not me he comes to see. It's my father.'

' No! Really? I don't believe it.'

' It's true. He practically ignores me.'

' He must be mad.'

Melanie shrugged. ' Not that I mind.'

' Sure?'

' Quite sure. He's a most unsettling, unpredictable person.'

' He's that all right,' agreed Eric. ' I would never have thought he would make friends with anyone who might be affected by a new motorway. But I'm glad it's your father he goes to see, otherwise my chances with you might be nil.'

' Why should you say that? You're as good a man

as he is, probably better.'

He gave a slow smile. 'That's very sweet of you. I only said it because—' he shrugged—'well, Drew Hamilton is the type who usually gets what he wants.'

And he doesn't want me. The thought flashed unbidden into Melanie's mind, and as swiftly she reacted against it. He didn't want her? She did not want *him* in any way whatsoever. Deliberately, she smiled up into Eric's face, and seizing his opportunity he kissed her swiftly. But somehow Melanie was aware of a sense of pain deep inside her. She did not speculate on the cause. She tried to ignore it. She hoped only that when she arrived home that night Drew would not be there.

She and Eric went to see a film in one of the Chesterfield cinemas, and feeling it was time she returned his hospitality she asked him home for coffee and sandwiches.

'What if my boss is there?' Eric enquired of her.

'Does it matter?' she returned, a suggestion of defiance in her tone.

'I don't mind if you don't.'

'That's all right, then.'

She pushed open the living room door, and with a sense of disappointment found it empty.

'That you, Richard?' her mother called from the kitchen.

'No, Mother—it's me.' Melanie invited Eric to sit down, then went through to her. 'Where's Father?'

'He and Drew have popped along to the local to replenish the lemonades and tonics. At least, that was their excuse,' she added with a smile.

'So they'll be coming back?' Melanie eyed the stack of sandwiches her mother was preparing.

'Well, dear, your father *does* live here,' her mother pointed out mildly.

And so does Drew, very nearly, Melanie almost answered.

'And Drew's coming back with him for a sandwich,'

64

finished her mother somewhat unnecessarily.

'Well, I've asked Eric in, too,' Melanie said resignedly.

'That's all right, dear, I'm glad you did. Here you are, take these in,' Helen added, putting two plates of sandwiches into her hands. 'I'll bring in the coffee. We won't wait. Anyhow, I should think they'll be back any minute.'

They were. No sooner had Melanie set down the sandwiches than in Drew and Richard walked. Richard greeted Eric and his daughter immediately, but Melanie thought she detected faint disapproval in Drew's expression as his glance swivelled from one to the other. Why disapproval? she wondered. If it was all right for him to be here surely it was all right, too, for Eric?

'Good evening, Melanie—Eric,' he said with formal politeness after a pause.

Eric answered him with a more informal 'Hello.' Melanie murmured a reply which was barely audible even to herself. For some reason her voice had suddenly become very husky.

But Drew appeared unconcerned whether she replied or not. Already he had his back to her, putting away the bottles in the cabinet.

Coffee was poured, sandwiches passed round and polite conversation was made. At least, that was the way it seemed to Melanie. Eric's manner was very guarded, Drew was distant, her father somewhat thoughtful, her mother concentrating on her duties as hostess, which she always took most seriously, and Melanie feeling anything but her natural self.

But presently Helen enquired brightly of Melanie and Eric: 'And what have you two been doing with yourselves this evening?' As it had been a very interesting and controversial film, the conversation brightened a little. It was not very long, however, before Drew rose to go, and Eric followed suit as if by honour bound. Melanie and her father showed them out.

'Good night—and thank you,' Drew called out, striding characteristically down the drive without lingering.

Eric gave Melanie a quick hug. 'Come for a run tomorrow evening?' he murmured as his lips brushed her cheek.

'Yes, all right,' answered Melanie hurriedly, giving a swift glance at Drew's receding back.

In the circumstances Eric did not linger either. With a final squeeze of her hand he followed in Drew Hamilton's footsteps.

Melanie turned to her father, but instead of waiting with her as he would have done normally he had gone straight indoors. She could have understood this if Eric had hung on, but he hadn't.

'Is anything wrong, Dad?' she asked later when her mother had gone to put out the milk bottles.

'Wrong?' he echoed swiftly. 'No. Why should there be?'

'You've been so quiet all evening. At least, since I came in.'

He shook his head. 'You're imagining things. Good night, Melanie.'

Her mother returned and Melanie followed her upstairs, leaving her father locking up and putting out the lights. It was when she was drawing back her curtains prior to getting into bed that she saw a figure at the coppice end of the garden. For a moment she was startled, thinking it might be an intruder—even a potential burglar. But as her eyes became accustomed to the darkness she could see it was her father. She slipped on her coat and a pair of casual shoes, then tiptoed downstairs and let herself quietly out of the house.

Richard swung round as she approached him. 'Melanie, what are you doing out here?'

'That's what I came to ask you, Dad,' she answered quietly. 'What's on your mind? Something is, I'm certain.'

He sighed. 'Perhaps there is—but that doesn't mean I'm going to tell you about it. At least, not yet.'

She eyed him worriedly. 'But—but, Dad, why? Are you ill? Are you worried about the business? But you can't be or I'd know. Is it anything to do with the motorway?'

He shook his head. 'Go to bed, Melanie—and not a word about any of this to your mother. I don't want her to start worrying. It's nothing, anyway. Can't a man have a few moments to himself without one or other of the women in his life bothering him? Off you go now. I'll be in in a moment.'

Melanie suppressed a sigh and went back indoors. It was the same old story. *Don't tell your mother.* It was all wrong. A man ought to confide in his wife. She should share his problems, not be protected from them. That was how she saw marriage. But why did he not want to confide in herself? He often did. Perhaps if she had been his son instead of his daughter— But maybe she was worrying needlessly. She would leave the matter for a day or two and see how he was then.

The day arrived when they were to run over with Drew to see the plot of land he was thinking of buying. Melanie was torn two ways about the trip. A part of her was curious and wanted to see it, the other part of her somehow shrank from seeing where he would probably live with his bride-to-be.

But why did it matter to her? she asked herself. Was it that she had reached the time in her own life when she wanted a home of her own? But she could have that to some extent any time she wanted. Many of her friends already had their own flats with furniture of their own choice. Some even in the very street where their parents lived. One did not have to marry to have a place of one's own. No, it was much more than that, she reasoned, more than just a place of her own. '*In the spring*,' according to Tennyson, '*a young man's fancy lightly turns to thoughts of love.'* So, she supposed, did a young woman's. Maybe that was it. It was spring, the time for falling in love, for weddings and orange blossom and the start of a new life in a new home with the man one loved.

'Melanie, Drew is here!' floated her mother's voice up the stairs.

Melanie shook herself out of her reverie. She had not even changed yet. As she never liked to keep people waiting, the navy slacks she was wearing would have to do. Drew considered that she dressed too well, anyway, she reflected ruefully. Swiftly, she pulled a white hand-knitted sweater over her head which covered completely the little white jumper she was wearing, and hastily smoothed her hair.

When she went downstairs everyone was outside. Melanie joined them, then stopped short.

Emerging from Drew's car and showing a very slim leg was a woman—tall, young, strikingly good-looking with well-groomed black hair and wearing a dress which could only be described as 'sweetly feminine'.

Melanie was shocked at the swift pang of jealousy which assailed her.

CHAPTER IV

On an involuntary impulse Melanie half turned to go into the house again, but was stopped in her tracks by a loud hail from Drew.

'Melanie, come and meet Stephanie.'

She turned slowly and descended the two steps from the front door. Drew was smiling in a way she had never seen before, extraordinarily pleased with himself.

'Melanie, this is Stephanie Holland. She's down from my home town for the week-end. Stephanie, meet Melanie Lawrence.'

Stephanie looked Melanie up and down, then a slow smile of amusement crossed her face. Melanie felt herself duly summed up as being far from a dangerous rival and dismissed. For her own part she was acutely aware of the casual way she was dressed in comparison with the other girl, and of the other's good looks. Neither made an effort to shake hands. Both said a brief 'hello'. Drew looked from one to the other, his arms folded and that odd smile on his face. Already having been introduced, it seemed, Helen and Richard stood looking on.

'Well, we'd better get going,' Drew said cheerfully.

'I think I'd better stay home,' volunteered Melanie swiftly. 'Five in one car will be something of a squeeze and it's hardly worth taking mine.'

'Nonsense. There's loads of room for three in the back—especially three slim ones like you and Stephanie and your father.'

'No, I—'

He took hold of her arm. 'What's the matter, Melanie? Something thrown you?'

She rounded on him angrily. 'What on earth are you talking about? I simply have no wish to be packed like a sardine.'

'Then follow in your own car—and bring Stephanie,' he said reasonably.

Melanie began to feel like a truculent child. Why had she said that about not wishing to be packed in the car like a sardine? It was not the sort of thing she minded in the least. Her parents were calling. If she said she did not want to go or had changed her mind, there would be more protestations and explanations. She went and got in the back of the car beside her father. Stephanie, on the other side, had elected to sit behind the driver's seat, and throughout the journey kept leaning forward to talk to Drew, excluding the other three. Then her father also leaned forward to talk to her mother and Melanie felt the complete odd man out.

But there was something far more important nagging her as she gazed through the window, apparently absorbed in the passing scenery. What was the matter with her? Why had she felt as she had at the sight of Stephanie? She was not given to petty jealousy.

The feeling of heaviness in her heart was due to something much deeper. It was centred around Drew. She wanted to mean something to him.

She was in love with him.

At first she rejected the idea, but she could not deny it for long. She loved him. He was all she had dreamed about in a man—strong, intelligent, interesting, and that indefinable something to which there was no name. She had been attracted to him the first time she had ever set eyes on him that morning looking into their shop window, when all she had received from him had been a cold glance of disapproval. Now Stephanie had arrived on the scene. What was the girl to him? Something very important, without doubt, for her to have travelled from the Lake District to see him—and this plot of land.

Melanie suddenly became aware that the car had stopped. They were on a hillside, the moors stretching way above them, and below a winding ribbon of water

70

which could only be the Derwent.

'All out, those who want to see where the future home of the Hamiltons is going to be,' came Drew's voice.

Melanie was the last to leave the car which Drew had parked on a convenient lay-by. He was pointing across the road to where there was a stile giving access to a footpath.

The air was pure and fresh, almost intoxicating, and there was not another house in sight anywhere. It was beautiful. Drew led the way, closely followed by Stephanie, who made a great to-do about getting over the stile and had to be almost lifted over by Drew.

Over the stile they followed a path running along the meadow parallel with the road, then by way of a five-barred gate to another field.

Here Drew halted and surveyed the terrain. 'What about this, then?' he asked triumphantly, his glance embracing them all.

'You—you mean all of it? Your building plot is the whole field?' demanded Richard in astonishment. 'Why, there must be all of twenty acres.'

'That's right. And it's mine for the asking.'

'Well!'

'Why not? It's the only way of making sure somebody doesn't build a row of houses in front of you, or worse still, a factory.'

'True,' agreed Richard. 'But isn't this grazing land?'

Drew nodded. 'It still will be—at least a part of it. I shall let a large slice of it to the farmer I'm hoping to buy it from.'

'Oh, but why?' Stephanie exclaimed. 'Cows are such smelly things.'

Drew laughed. 'You wouldn't get close enough to them to smell them—unless you wanted to—which seemingly you wouldn't.'

The view was superb. Melanie imagined sitting at a

meal in Drew's house and looking out on to the sweep of meadow and lawns, the swiftly moving river, the wide sky, and beyond to the purple moors. A sharp flash of pain ran through her. Such heaven was hardly likely to be hers.

Drew turned to her. 'Well, Melanie, what do you think?'

'Does it matter what I think?' she returned quickly.

'Of course it does, otherwise I wouldn't have asked you. What about the view? Better than Hillrise, wouldn't you say?'

Melanie affected a careless shrug. She couldn't possibly give voice to what she was really thinking.

'Views aren't everything,' she said stiffly.

Drew gave her a keen look. 'I agree. But I thought you set a great deal of store by them.'

'Not more than ordinary. I love the country, of course, very much. And I love the view from Hillrise. But I wouldn't necessarily say that this is better.'

'You'd miss your fairy lights down in the valley, I suppose,' he said mockingly.

'Oh, Melanie,' protested her father, 'there's really no comparison. This is absolutely marvellous. Don't you agree, Helen?' he added turning to his wife.

'It's beautiful,' she agreed. 'But I know what Melanie means. It's more than just a view we see from Hillrise.'

'And you wouldn't change that for this?'

Helen laughed. 'I'm not being asked to, am I? But what does Stephanie think?'

That, Melanie thought with a pang, was more to the point. Stephanie had said very little so far. Now, four pairs of eyes were focussed upon the girl Drew was to marry.

'Oh, it's—it's lovely,' she said swiftly. 'But won't it be a bit isolated in the winter? I mean—there's not another house in sight anywhere.'

'Some people would think that was the beauty of it,' Drew said drily.

'And you're hardly isolated these days with things like the telephone and the car,' Richard Lawrence pointed out.

'But what if you get snowbound and the wires are down and—'

Drew gave her an amused look. 'I thought you were romantic, Stephanie. Wouldn't you like to be marooned—isolated with the man you love?'

At this she smiled coyly. 'With you, yes, Drew. You know that.'

Melanie did not wait to hear his answer to this. She ran down the hill towards the river, afraid of giving away what was in her heart. She should never have come. It was a beautiful spot, and married to a man like Drew—

She stared at the swiftly moving water, rushing on its journey from the mountains to the sea like a young wife rushing to meet her husband after a separation. She had been near to being in love many times, but had never before felt this tumult in her heart.

Then suddenly Drew was at her side. 'Why did you run away, Melanie?'

'I didn't. I just came to look at the river.'

'You like water?'

'Of course. Who doesn't?'

'Not everyone.'

Drew looked back up the hill, and his gaze was that of someone who had a vision, a dream of something special.

'A man could build a place up there that would be really worthwhile,' he said.

'Like Haddon Hall or Chatsworth?' she said mockingly to hide the tumult of her heart.

'In a way—yes,' he answered. 'Why not? This is a perfect site for a landscape garden. Lawns and terraces. Not a lake, perhaps, but a water garden or

73

pool.'

Melanie was beginning to see it, too, as if with eyes that were not her own but his.

'Ah yes.'

She suddenly remembered a photograph she had seen and by which she had been very much attracted. 'But not the conventional oblong or kidney-shaped pool. Not a swimming pool either.'

He gave her a swift glance. 'What, then? Tell me.'

She smiled. 'A long and narrow pool. About say— twenty or thirty feet long and only about six feet wide, with water lilies, irises and other aquatic plants, and hundreds of fish—large and small, blue and gold—'

'And pixies and dwarfs, little gnomes fishing—things like that?' he retaliated gently.

'Certainly not!'

'I was joking, of course,' he murmured. 'But go on. You'd set this long narrow pool of yours in a lawn, I expect?'

'No, I wouldn't, actually. I'd surround it with coloured paving and have small trees and flowering shrubs to form a varied background. A feature on its own, something people would come across suddenly, unexpectedly. A place where one could sit for a while and dream. A place of peace and seclusion.'

For a moment she was lost in her own dream world, seeing herself sitting there, quiet, relaxed and happy, gazing into the green depths of the pool, and beside her, his hand in hers—

Swiftly she turned away from the vision, only to meet the eyes of Drew fixed upon her reflectively.

'You know, you have some very good ideas,' he said slowly. 'How about helping me to design the place— house, gardens, the lot?'

She stared at him. 'You're not serious.'

'I certainly am. Why shouldn't I be?'

'But doesn't it concern Stephanie? Shouldn't she be

the one to help you?'

He gave a faint smile. 'I don't think it's much use my relying on Stephanie for ideas. Besides, she isn't on the spot, you are.'

'Surely one doesn't need to be "on the spot"?'

She couldn't understand him. The way he had spoken to Stephanie on the hill, and his not denying just now that the building of the house did concern her, all pointed to her being his future wife. Melanie would have thought any engaged couple would derive a great deal of joy and happiness from planning and designing a house and garden, especially one such as Drew had in mind. She couldn't possibly do as he suggested. It would be too ironical—and much, much too painful.

'I think one does,' Drew answered her. 'Especially once the building starts. Planning every small detail on paper is difficult—if not impossible. You have to allow for changes of mind and fresh ideas as the building proceeds.'

'But you won't be in the area much longer yourself,' she protested.

'As to that—who knows? I may not be far away. It depends on a number of things.'

Into whose land the greedy jaws of the motorway were next going to bite? she wondered somewhat bitterly. She answered coolly, 'I suppose so,' and turned to go back up the hill to rejoin the others. But as her gaze travelled upwards, once again the vision of a house and gardens sprang into her mental vision and she halted.

'The garden would have to be terraced, naturally. I can see green tiers, great stone vases, steps leading to the various levels—'

'And rockeries?'

'No, not rockeries. Green banks splashed in the spring with bright yellow daffodils. Oh, and thousands of daffodils at the river's edge as there are beside the Lakes in your part of the country.'

75

'Ah yes, a very nice picture,' murmured Drew. 'We'll do that. The farmer can have a piece of land on either side of the plot for his own purpose. This land will divide into three and still leave ample space for—our purpose.'

It certainly would to Melanie's modest standards and upbringing, but she could not resist another little thrust.

'I would have thought a man of your ambitions would have the whole meadow. Then you could *really* landscape it. You could plant beautiful trees like the blue cedar and other lovely conifers. And beech and chestnut—'

He nodded soberly. 'I could, but there are other considerations besides the realising of one's ambitions. There'll be plenty of room for trees as it is. Besides, cattle grazing on either side will add to the rural scene, don't you think? But what about the house? How do you see that—in brick or stone?'

'Oh, Derbyshire stone out here. Built square and plain with large windows from which you can step straight out into the garden without having to go all round the house as it were. And a large paved terrace where one could have meals outdoors in the summer.'

The corners of Drew's mouth curved. 'How would you like a stone balcony outside your bedroom window so that you could step straight out in the mornings in your negligée—or even have breakfast there?'

'Marvellous. That's something I've always dreamed about,' she answered without thinking. For a brief moment she felt a confusion of emotions grip her, but she recovered herself swiftly.

'I can see you're the outdoor type,' Drew said wryly, 'But perhaps a heated conservatory would have more frequent use in our unpredictable climate.'

'That, too,' she answered, giving him a wicked glance. 'I'm afraid if you give me a free hand I shall run you straight into bankruptcy.'

'Some things may take a little longer, that's all,' he said easily.

'I've heard that story somewhere before,' she told him with a touch of cynicism. 'In fact I remember seeing a cartoon once. A man in his shirt sleeves was sitting outside his home with a friend. His home consisted of four Doric pillars and behind them a house which was little more than a shack. The caption: " Yes, I had all kinds of ideas when I started to build this place ".'

'And you think that my ideas—and yours—would evaporate once the foundations were dug?'

'They might if their fulfilment took too long.'

'You underestimate me. Once I've fixed my mind on a thing I don't let go so easily.'

Melanie could well believe it. 'I think we should join the others,' she said.

She started up the hill, then was brought to a halt as he gripped her arm.

'You haven't given a firm answer to my question. Will you help me? Most houses suffer from not having a woman's ideas in the planning of them.'

'I suppose you mean in the kitchen?' she flashed back.

'*Not* just the kitchen. I wouldn't want my wife to spend half her life—or anything near it—in the kitchen unless she really wanted to. And I would hope she would have better things to occupy her time, anyway, than spend hours preparing food, cooking it, helping to eat it, and then washing up after it.'

'I'm glad to hear you say that. But I can't understand you. I would have thought the right person to help you plan any part of this house of yours would be the woman you're going to marry.'

'I'm asking *you*,' he insisted in a quiet, decisive voice, but giving nothing away.

But why me? she wanted to argue. Then all at once

77

she knew she *wanted* to help Drew plan his home.

' All right,' she told him. . ' But remember—my name isn't Capability Brown.'

' Ah! The famous eighteenth-century landscape gardener who planned so many of the gardens of England's stately homes—including Chatsworth.'

' That's right.'

' But I don't suppose he had a clue about the layout of a house.'

' How do you know I have?'

' I'm backing a hunch,' he said.

When they reached the top of the hill again only Richard and Helen were there.

' Where's Stephanie?' enquired Drew.

' Gone back to the car,' Richard answered. ' She got tired of waiting. What have you two been talking about down there, may one ask?' he added lightly.

' Oh, exchanging ideas about architecture and land-scape gardening,' Drew answered. ' Melanie is going to help me design my house and plan the garden layout.'

' Is she indeed?' Richard murmured.

But he sounded only mildly surprised, and Melanie noticed that her mother showed none at all. She simply couldn't understand it.

When they joined Stephanie in the car, Drew apolo-gised at once for keeping her waiting. Her disgruntled expression gave way to a smile readily. Melanie had half expected some show of jealousy or annoyance to be directed against herself, but there was none. How sure she must be of him, she thought dismally.

Of the rest of that day Melanie remembered little. Her mind was much too painfully occupied with unhappy thoughts of her own. She was in love with a man who already was planning to build a house for his bride-to-be. What could be more hopeless? She had been a fool to agree to help him. A fool. But she knew per-fectly well that she would go on being a fool. She *wanted* to have a hand in the planning of Drew's house. She could not help it. She was like a rabbit hypnotised by the lights of an oncoming car, she told herself. She knew it would be painful, when ultimately some other woman would be living there with him, and yet she wanted to do it. She wanted to do it because Drew wanted her to. Could any woman be more hopelessly in love than that?

She was almost relieved when the following day Eric came into the shop and suggested they might go to a country club for dinner where there was also dancing. In Eric's cheerful company she might at least forget Drew for a time. But even that proved impossible. Drew had already become a living part of her.

At last, as if divining her thoughts, Eric asked her what she had been doing over the week-end. He himself had been home. So naturally enough she told him about the excursion to see Drew's plot of land. Eric grimaced.

'I told you he was a dark horse. He's never said a word to me about settling down here—or about getting married. I should think it came as a surprise to you and your parents, didn't it?'

'Well, yes, but—'

'He's a man who acts first and tells you afterwards.'

'You could equally say he's a man who keeps his own counsel,' Melanie pointed out, inwardly nettled by Eric's criticism of Drew.

'You could put it that way,' Eric answered sarcastically. 'I saw this girl Stephanie, by the way. I wondered who she was. Drew said nothing about her, of course. I thought she looked quite something—but not Hamilton's type at all.'

'That doesn't sound very complimentary towards Drew. Anyway, the most unlikely and apparently ill-assorted couples often make a perfectly happy marriage.'

She forced herself to say it. But it was as though they were talking about someone else, not about Drew

79

whom she loved.

'You think they're engaged?' asked Eric.

'Well, he'd obviously brought her along to see his building plot.'

'And did she like it—the situation, I mean?'

'I think she was a bit put off by the remoteness, but of course—'

'She was content to be where *he* wanted to be. Right?'

Melanie nodded. She wished they had never started the conversation and searched her mind for some other topic, but Eric went on:

'That's typical of the man. Everyone has to fit in with what *he* wants.'

Melanie frowned. 'You sound as though you really dislike him.'

'Isn't that the way he has struck you?' Eric persisted. 'Fond of having his own way?'

'Well—' In a way it was true, she mused. Drew was a man who knew what he wanted. A man of action, of strong opinions. It was so easy to let such a man have his own way. Certainly Stephanie had not been very enamoured of Drew's site for a house. Yet he was bent on going ahead with it. With a man like him for a husband one would either have to be submissive or be forever asserting one's rights—which could lead to quarrels and bitterness. There was so much about Drew she admired, quite apart from being in love with him, but did the ideal man really exist, the one who could be strong, manly, and at the same time gentle and pliable, especially with the woman he loved? Or was that a contradiction of character? Then she recalled his swift apology to Stephanie. Perhaps he *was* all of these things, after all, she thought with a pang.

'I don't know what makes women fall for a man like that,' Eric was saying.

Melanie took a deep breath. She had no wish to

quarrel with Eric, and if she showed any resentment to his remarks or defended Drew too warmly he might guess how she felt about him, and she did not want that.

So she returned: 'But surely an equal number fall for you? Or maybe even more.'

He darted a swift look at her. 'You think so?'

'Why not? You're easy to talk to, to get to know. Whereas Drew can be—difficult.'

'I know! That's what galls me sometimes.' Then he smiled. 'But let's talk about something more pleasant. Obviously *you* haven't fallen for him.'

Melanie did not contradict him. Eric talked, but she hardly heard him. She was thinking still of Drew, the deeply rooted desire in him to create something great for the woman he loved, and could barely suppress a groan. But Eric and she alternately danced and ate and talked, and the evening passed for Melanie in a haze of unreality. The real part of her was with Drew.

When they drove home Eric invited her to his caravan for a late-night coffee and Melanie agreed. It had become a habit to round off an evening in this way, but more usually it was at Melanie's home. Tonight, however, Melanie did not want to run the risk of Drew being at home. As it was, she noticed that his caravan was in darkness.

It was when they were waiting for the kettle to boil that Eric threw out casually:

'We're nearly at the end of our work in this immediate area.'

Melanie felt her heart give a sudden downward plunge. 'Where—will you go next?' he jerked out.

'I'm not sure yet.' Eric reached into a cupboard for two cups and saw the expression on her face which she had been unable to hide. 'Hey, I really believe you're sorry we're going.' He put an arm about her shoulders. '*Will* you miss me, Melanie?'

'Yes, of course I shall miss you,' she answered rather absently. She was recalling how Drew had hinted that they might not be far away. All the same, he would not be dropping in at home so often, she thought regretfully.

Quite suddenly, however, Eric's arms came about her and before she could do anything about it he was kissing her in a way she did not want to be kissed by any man except Drew.

She averted her face and pushed against him. 'Eric—don't, please.'

'Oh, come on—'

'No! Let me go!' she said sharply.

His hands dropped to his sides. 'Sorry. I *thought* you liked me.'

'I do, but—'

'Say no more. I've got the message, I think.'

Clearly, she had offended him. It would be an embarrassment now to stay for coffee.

'I'd better go, Eric, if you don't mind. We've a busy day at the bookshop tomorrow and I must catch up on some sleep.'

He dropped the tin of coffee down on the table with a clatter. 'All right, I'll walk you to the house.'

'No, no—there's no need. It's a bright night and I know the way blindfold.'

She went out swiftly before he could argue. The light was now on in Drew's caravan. As she passed, he appeared at the window and flicked the curtain across with a rough, decisive movement. She stood frozen for a moment, feeling utterly bereft. The act was symbolic, as if he were shutting her out of his life. She shivered and forced herself to move. It was all her imagination, of course. She didn't suppose for a moment that he had even seen her. In a lighted room one cannot see outside in the darkness except for a few yards, and she had not been all that close.

Disconsolately, she let herself into the house, and as soon as she reasonably could, escaped to her room and her own unhappy thoughts.

She did not see Drew for quite a number of days, and she was convinced that he had not been really serious when he had asked her help in designing his house and gardens. All the same, she could not stop herself from thinking about it. She became obsessed with planning and sketching, using sheet after sheet of paper. Her own dream house. She realised that as well as knowing the folly of it all. She drew a ground floor plan which had a lounge hall, an elegantly curved staircase, a cloakroom, a study for Drew and a music room for herself with an additional piano in the large lounge. Her imagination ran riot. There would be a guest suite, a nursery, and a private bathroom with twin washbasins for Drew and herself. There would be a cedarwood summer house down by the river, they would have a boat—

Swiftly she crumpled up the plan into a light ball and flung it into the wastepaper basket, only to start again after a few minutes.

Eric appeared in the office unannounced one day as she was drawing a plan for the garden.

'What on earth are you doing?' he said in an amused voice. 'Got a new hobby?'

She snatched up the piece of paper and tore it into shreds. 'Just doodling.'

'Well, come out and have lunch with me.'

More because she was caught off guard than from a great desire for his company she accepted, then later wished she hadn't because Drew was having lunch in the same restaurant. He was sitting alone at a small table near the window, and she half expected him to cross over and speak to them, but he finished his meal and left with barely a second glance in their direction.

Eric's gaze followed him. 'If he were not so good at his job I'd put in a request not to work with him again,' he muttered. 'He's been quite unbearable lately.'

'In what way?' asked Melanie.

'Oh, nothing you can lay your finger on. Just—uncommunicative. Difficult.'

Melanie could well accept this, but made no further comment.

'See you tonight?' asked Eric as they rose after the meal.

'Sorry. It's my music lesson.'

He grimaced. 'You're a funny girl. Why do you still have lessons when you can play so well?'

'Oh, there's always something to learn,' she answered evasively.

She looked forward to what she called her 'music nights'. She was at present learning Grieg's piano concerto, and the more she played it under the tuition of her music master the more excited she became about it. Hearing wonderful music like that was thrilling enough, but to be able to play it oneself really well—She longed for the day when she was ready to perform it in public, even though she only performed as an amateur.

She did not explain to Eric, however. He would not understand. Drew would, of course. He would know exactly what she meant.

It was strange that the more she yearned for a sight of Drew the more she saw of Eric. He would call often in the shop and ask her out to lunch or for an evening meal. She wished he wouldn't, yet found it difficult to refuse his invitations too often. He would call at the house, too, sometimes being there when she arrived home.

'Don't you have a job these days?' she quizzed him, laughing, on one such occasion, though in actual fact she was not very amused. She did not enjoy Eric's company very much now. She did not like the way he often spoke of Drew, nor had she liked the way he had kissed her that evening in his caravan.

'Work in this area is slackening off now,' he answered.
'Besides, can you blame me for wanting to see more of
you?'

Here Melanie's mother intervened. 'If your work is
slackening off, does that mean your survey in the immediate area is nearly finished?'

He nodded. 'Any day now we expect to get our
"marching orders".'

A small, uncertain frown appeared on Helen's brow.
'That's odd. Drew didn't say anything. But then we
haven't seen him for a day or so.'

Eric smiled faintly. 'Drew never lets his left hand
know what his right hand is doing.'

'People in authority often appear to be like that,'
Helen answered tartly. 'At least, those who are any
good.'

She went out and Eric looked after her ruefully.
'Your mother is decidedly pro-Drew, isn't she?'

Melanie felt irritated. 'I don't know why you should
say that. It suggests that she's anti-someone else and
she isn't.'

He grinned. 'We'll skip it. Come along to my place
and I'll cook up a meal, then we can go to see a film.'

But this time she shook her head. 'Not tonight, Eric,
thanks. I have things I *must* do.'

'Such as washing your hair?' he quizzed.

'No, not washing my hair.'

Actually, her parents were going out to dinner on this
particular evening, and she wanted to take full advantage
of having the house to herself to practise some of the
more difficult passages of the concerto. Though her
parents were musical themselves and understood the need
for practice, it could not be very pleasant listening to
someone repeating the same bar or phrase over and over
again, and Melanie was always conscious of this.

'Sure you won't change your mind?' asked Eric.

'Quite sure.'

Her mind already on the music she saw him off and could scarcely wait for her parents to go out.

She had played for a full hour and rose only to switch on the light when the front door bell rang. In a fever of impatience against the interruption she went to open it, and her heart leapt to find Drew standing there.

He looked rather surprised to see her. 'Hello, Melanie. Your father home?'

'No, I'm afraid he isn't. He and Mother have gone out to dinner with friends.'

'Oh, I see.'

'Won't you come in for a few minutes?' she asked.

He hesitated for a fraction, then said 'thank you', and stepped inside. 'Actually, I thought you'd be out.'

'Is that why you came?' she found herself flashing back.

'No,' he answered briefly. Then he said: 'I wonder if you'll come for a short run with me? There's something I'd like to show you.'

She couldn't refuse him. She could not refuse Drew anything. Her practising of the concerto would have to wait.

'I'll get my coat,' she said, wondering what it was he wanted to show her, and experiencing a thrill of happiness at the unexpected contact with him.

To her surprise he drove her down into the valley where one by one lights were being switched on in the houses. In the middle of the row of cottages called Mill Lane he stopped the car. Some of the houses were still in semi-darkness, but many of the curtains were still undrawn and she could see the glow of the fires from within.

'I suspect these old people delay switching on the lights for as long as possible in the belief that they are being economical,' Drew observed.

'I suppose so.' Melanie gave him a puzzled look.

Why had he brought her here?

'I've spoken to some of them,' Drew went on. 'The cottages might not be much by some standards, but these people are happy in this valley.'

'I'm sure they are.'

What was he trying to say? Through the window of one of the cottages Melanie could see an elderly woman setting the table for supper; in another, a couple were watching television.

'It would be a cardinal sin to uproot them,' Drew said quietly.

Melanie turned to him swiftly. 'Is there any danger? —I mean—'

'There's no danger,' he answered in the same low voice.

She stared at him. 'You—you mean the motorway is going along the top of the hill, after all—through our house?'

He nodded gravely. 'That's what I came to tell your parents—before they hear it from the official source.'

Even though she knew he had been trying to prepare her for the news, Melanie was stunned for a moment. She had no wish to see these old people turned out of their homes, naturally, but—A terrible feeling of loss, of deprivation swamped her as she thought of her own home.

'I—I simply can't believe it,' she said slowly.

Drew turned to her. 'But, Melanie, surely you knew there was a possibility? Changes happen in everybody's life at some time or other. You have to learn to accept them.'

'Learn to accept seeing your home in ruins? And all for the sake of a road to take more and yet more traffic?'

'It's hard, I know. But, Melanie, *you* have a car, haven't you?'

'I need it.'

'That's what everyone says. But would you be willing to give yours up in order to make one car less on the roads? You don't *really* need one. There's a perfectly good bus service which stops within a few yards of your house. And of course, your father has a car.'

Melanie's lips tightened angrily. It was all so true, but that did not make her feel better about things in the slightest.

'It is so terribly easy to be reasonable about someone else's problems, Drew. Would you mind taking me home now, please?'

Drew gave her a swift look, then without a word he started the car.

'Will you come in and wait for my parents?' she asked politely when he drew up outside the front door of Hillrise.

'No, I think not, thanks. Perhaps I'd better call back. I regret having to spoil their evening out by giving them news which I'm sure will upset them—especially your mother. Your father was forewarned. All the same, the news will break tomorrow and I would rather they heard it from me, unpleasant though the task will be. I can't really leave it to you, either.'

'All right,' Melanie said tonelessly. 'Come back about ten o'clock. That's usually the time they arrive home mid-week from a dinner engagement.'

She let herself into the house, a mixture of feelings. How could he? she thought unreasonably. How could he have allowed this to happen when he had been so friendly with her parents? It seemed like a betrayal. Her mother and father would not like being uprooted any more than those people down in the valley. Neither would she herself.

She went upstairs and stood at the window of her room to gaze down at her beloved valley. This view and this house symbolized security. To leave it would be a wrench of the first magnitude. But as her eyes filled with tears it was Drew's lighted caravan upon which they were focussing.

Soon after her parents arrived home Drew rang the front doorbell. Melanie was making hot drinks and listening to her mother's account of the evening spent with their friends. It was her father who went to the door and brought Drew into the kitchen.

'One more cup of coffee, Melanie. Drew has something to tell us. We'll go through into the other room if you don't mind.'

'Sounds mysterious,' Helen said. 'What can it be, I wonder?'

Melanie picked up the tray of drinks. 'Let's go in and find out.'

Melanie suspected that her father either already knew or had guessed. It was her mother who pressed Drew to tell his news.

'I'm afraid it's not very good, Mrs Lawrence,' Drew began. 'But I feel sure you won't be upset for long.'

'What is it, for goodness' sake?'

Drew came straight to the point. 'It's about the motorway. The news will be public by tomorrow. You —will have to find another house. But you *will* be compensated, of course.'

Melanie watched the colour drain from her mother's face. 'I—I don't quite understand, Drew. Do—do you mean to say that the motorway is actually going to run through Hillrise, through our house?'

He ventured a smile. 'Well, along the ground where your house now stands. But you'll have plenty of time to look around for another one, or even have one built. And you'll be well compensated.'

'Compensated?' Helen looked at him blankly. 'How can one be compensated for a bulldozer going through one's home? Oh, Drew—Richard—this is unbelievable!'

Richard crossed to her side swiftly. 'Now, Helen, you're not to get upset. Once you get used to the idea you'll enjoy choosing a new house.'

Helen's lips quivered and Melanie could see that tears were not very far away.

'I don't want a new house. I like this one.'

Melanie took a deep breath. 'Mother, you—we all of us knew this might happen, and we've got to face it.'

Helen looked at her through a veil of tears. 'You're wrong there, Melanie, I didn't think for a moment it would happen. I quite thought Drew would—'

'I'm sorry, Mrs Lawrence,' Drew came in. 'But I *did* tell you I had no influence and I tried to prepare you.'

'You said you had no idea—and of course you have influence,' Helen said tearfully. 'You send in your report, don't you? And the powers that be base their decision on that.'

Drew rose. 'I had to send in a true report, Mrs Lawrence,' he said quietly. 'But I'm sure you'll feel differently when you've had time to think about it and to get used to the idea. I'll come and see you again in a day or two, if I may—and I might even have a suggestion to make about a new house for you.'

Melanie saw him to the door. 'You knew all along where the motorway was going to run, didn't you?' she challenged. 'That's why you thought it safe to make friends with my parents.'

'That was *not* the reason why I became friendly with you and your parents. I had formed an opinion, yes,' he admitted, 'based on my knowledge as a civil engineer and my experience of motorways, but obviously you're in no mood to listen to reason.'

'It's easy to be reasonable when the problem doesn't concern you!' she flashed back.

He gripped her shoulders fiercely. 'Of course it concerns me, you little idiot. I told your father how it might be some time ago. I'd have told your mother, too, but he asked me not to. He assured me that *you'd* be sensible about it. How wrong he was. And how wrong *I* was about you, too.'

He let her go abruptly and without even saying good-night, strode to his car and drove off.

Melanie stood there for a moment, on the brink of tears herself. But her tears were not at the thought of leaving Hillrise, they were on Drew's account. Why she had spoken to him as she had? She knew perfectly well it wasn't Drew's fault that the motorway was going to eat its way through their home. She had hit out at him simply because of the frustration of being in love with him. She couldn't help it. His calling unexpectedly at the house had thrown her off balance. He had disapproved of her from the very beginning. Now he thought her week and spineless, one who could not face the hard knocks of life.

Oh, Drew!

CHAPTER V

When Drew had gone Melanie would have given anything to go straight up to her room, but she knew she would be expected to join her parents. As she had anticipated, her father was trying to comfort her mother, telling her about the lovely new house they could have.

'I don't want a new house. I like this one,' came the near-childish answer.

Richard sighed wearily and glanced helplessly at Melanie. 'I'll clear away these things,' he said, and began to collect the coffee cups together.

Melanie went and sat beside her mother. 'Look, darling, I know how you feel, but nothing can alter it, so we might as well try to accept it *now* as be miserable for days on end.'

She couldn't help thinking that if her father had not tried to protect her mother and had told her earlier, she might by this time have already accepted it. She recalled vividly now, the night she had discovered him alone in the garden late at night. Was that when Drew had told him there was a strong possibility—a certainty—that the motorway would cut through their land?

'I'm—so disappointed in Drew—' wailed Helen. 'I really did think he was on our side.'

'Mother, it has nothing to do with his "being on our side". He simply has a job to do. I—I know it's difficult to accept changes and I know it's more difficult for you than it is for me, but we both knew it *might* happen.'

'You may have done, but I didn't.'

'Only because you won't face things, Mother.'

Miraculously, anger dried Helen's tears. 'How dare you speak to me like that, Melanie!'

'I'm sorry, Mother, but it's the truth. Father has

always tried to protect you—and he shouldn't have. It doesn't help.'

'My own daughter—telling her parents how they should behave!' Helen deplored, her blue eyes wide with reproach.

'I don't mean it that way, Mother,' Melanie answered patiently. 'I'm just being honest. Come along, let's go to bed. There's nothing to be gained by talking any more tonight.'

The morning's mail brought a letter from the Council confirming Drew's news, and a few days later a young man called to discuss compensation. They had six months in which to find another house.

'But not nearly enough time to build,' deplored Richard, ' and we've still got to find a plot. Of course, we *could* look around for one already built, but—'

Drew had called as promised. He had not made any further mention of Melanie helping him design his house, and she was not at all surprised. She was quite sure in her own mind that he had not made the suggestion seriously.

He said now in reply to Richard: 'That need not be any problem. I'd be more than happy for you to have a piece of my land. We can make it a pair of houses, if you like, looking as though they belong, yet separate. One for me and one for you.'

'You—you really mean that?' asked Richard with obvious relief.

Drew nodded. 'In fact two houses will look better than one. And with the summer ahead a house *can* be ready in six months. But by far the best plan is to be your own builder—that way you can control the pace, pay overtime rates if you can afford to.'

'But I'm not a builder!' Richard protested. 'I don't know the first thing about building houses.'

'You don't have to be a builder. You simply employ those who *do* know—bricklayers, carpenters and so on,

93

and buy your own materials. You simply register as the builder—which you would be in effect.'

Richard shook his head. ' I have a business to attend to. Besides, I wouldn't know how many bricks to order, how much timber, how many bags of cement or anything.'

' There are books on the subject,' Drew insisted. ' And I would help you. I've got a long holiday coming, and even when I start work again I could park my caravan on the building site and drive to wherever I'm going to be working. I—have a feeling it won't be very far from here. Being your own builder is as much a matter of paper-work as anything and seeing to it that time and materials are not wasted. The two houses could be built more or less at the same time, so that if progress is held up on one for any reason, the men could proceed with the other, because once workmen go away to another site it's not always easy to get them back again. That's where so many delays are caused and why building a house often takes so long. Surely one of you —either yourself or Melanie—could be spared from the bookshop? Summer is coming. *Do* people read as much in the summer? I doubt it.'

At first Melanie had felt some dismay at the idea of living next door to Drew with Stephanie as his wife, but now she could not help the thrill of excitement which began to stir within her. It would be wonderful to see a house being built stage by stage and above all to be working side by side with Drew.

' Father, let's do it—that is, if Mother thinks it a good idea, too. I'll help. I don't want a holiday this year. You—you could even spare me away from the shop—except on Saturdays, of course. And on Saturdays I shouldn't think the workmen will want to work either.'

' That's true,' Drew put in. ' There's sport on Saturdays, you see. Many of them would rather work Sundays than Saturdays.'

Richard looked at Melanie as if she'd taken leave of her senses.

'But you know even less about the business of building a house than I do. It's—it's ridiculous. What do you think, Helen?' he asked, turning to his wife.

'Well, since you ask me, I think the whole idea is a very good one. If we've got to move—and it seems we must, why then I'd much rather have a new house and plan it as we want it, and as Drew obviously knows something about building and Melanie is willing to help —I think we should let them go ahead.'

Melanie could barely hide her astonishment. 'You mean that, Mother?'

'Of course I mean it. Why shouldn't I?'

'But—but when we went to look at Drew's plot you said—'

'Do stop arguing, Melanie. I can change my mind, can't I?'

Her husband had sat rather dumbfounded. Melanie passed him a smile of amusement. 'Well, Father? What do you say now?' she asked.

He shook his head. 'I give up. At three to one the odds are too much for me. If you and Drew are sure—'

'We're sure,' they answered in unison.

'Then what's the first step? I'll do all I can to help, of course.'

At this point there was a ring at the front door. 'I'll go,' Helen said. 'But don't make any vital decisions until I get back.'

Drew said that the first step was for him to sell a building plot to Richard and at the same time get planning permission for the other house.

'Meanwhile, maybe Melanie and Mrs Lawrence can get their heads together on the designing. An architect will draw the plans from their rough design, and these will have to be submitted to the local council.' He turned to Melanie. 'Did you get anywhere with a design for my place?'

'Well, I—'

She stopped as her mother appeared in the doorway with Eric. She had almost forgotten his existence.

'Eric has come to say goodbye,' Helen said.

Eric's glance went swiftly to Drew, who gave him an unsmiling look. 'Well, goodbye for the present, anyway. I certainly hope to see you all again before long,' he said, his smile actually directed at Melanie.

'When are you leaving the area, then?' she asked.

'Oh, some time tomorrow. I—wanted to say, too, how sorry I am about your house. If I could have done anything to prevent the motorway coming up here I would.'

Helen invited him to sit down. 'Thank you, Eric, but we've more or less become reconciled—and Drew has just made the most marvellous suggestion.'

'Oh?'

Eagerly now, Helen put Eric in the picture. He grimaced and gave Drew an odd, sideways glance. 'I thought that plot of land you bought was a little big even for your extravagant taste—and Stephanie's. But of course, you've done this sort of thing before, haven't you?'

'What sort of thing?' Drew asked sharply.

Eric smiled faintly as if secretly enjoying himself. 'Why—buying up land and then selling it in lots at a profit. I wish I could afford to do it. You must make quite a bit of money that way.'

Drew's jaw tigthtened. He rose to his feet. 'If you'll excuse me, Mrs Lawrence—all of you—I have a lot of tidying up to do. I'll see my solicitor, Richard, and have an agreement drawn up. Perhaps, if you wouldn't mind seeing me out, we can talk about the price and how much land you'd like.'

Eric grinned at Drew's back, then said, when the two men had gone from the room:

'He didn't like that, did he?'

Neither Melanie nor her mother spoke for a minute, then Helen rose. 'Excuse me, Eric, I have to see about lunch.'

Eric looked after her ruefully. 'I'm afraid I've put my foot in it again. Sorry.'

'You've certainly broken up a happy and pleasant discussion,' Melanie told him, feeling wretched about what he had said concerning Drew. 'We were under the impression that Drew was doing us a favour in letting us have a slice of his land.'

'Drew is an opportunist,' declared Eric.

'I thought you said you didn't know him very well,' Melanie flashed back.

He grunted. 'I'm learning. Really, Melanie, don't you think it's too much of a coincidence that Drew should *happen* to have bought that land and then the motorway should *happen* to be ploughing a way through your house?'

Melanie stared at him. 'What on earth are you implying?'

'Figure it out for yourself,' he answered with a shrug. 'Who is in a better position to know that *somebody* is going to need a new house when a motorway is going to zip through their living room—or where it used to be?'

Melanie felt herself go cold all over. 'I—I simply don't believe it.'

Eric put his hand on her shoulder. 'I'm sorry. It's never very pleasant to be disillusioned about somebody. Anyway, what does it matter? He's solved your parents' problem, hasn't he?'

'Yes, he has done that,' Melanie answered tonelessly.

'Well, cheer up. Come out and have lunch with me. We're moving off first thing in the morning. I shan't be able to see quite so much of you.'

She shook her head swiftly. 'No, no—thanks all the same. I—have to go out.'

She hadn't intended to. It was Sunday and she had planned to cut out a new dress for her next concert. But now she felt she must get out. Anywhere. Anywhere to be alone. She went into the kitchen. 'Mother, I'm going out for a little while.'

Helen swung around from the cooker. 'With Eric? You'll be in to lunch?'

'No, Mother, I won't be in to lunch, but I'll probably be back for tea. Perhaps you'd like to go and say goodbye to Eric while I get my coat.'

She went upstairs. When she came down again her mother had returned to the kitchen and her father was standing with Eric in the hall at the front door shaking hands. Melanie opened it, anxious to get away.

'Goodbye, then, Eric. Come and see us again,' Richard said.

'I certainly will.' Outside, Eric said to Melanie, 'Sure you won't change your mind?'

She shook her head; she did not want particularly to see Eric ever again.

'I'll say goodbye now. I—shall be very busy this summer, so I doubt if I shall be able to see much of you even if you come over.'

'What will you be doing? Building a house?'

'In effect, yes.'

He laughed. 'Watch out for Stephanie. She can be quite madly jealous.'

'She has nothing to be jealous about as far as I'm concerned,' Melanie answered swiftly.

'No? Well, I'm glad to hear that. 'Bye for the present, Melanie—and I *shall* be seeing you.'

Melanie took a deep breath and got into her car. What he had said about Drew couldn't be true. It just couldn't. It was unthinkable that he should be making profit out of other people's distresses and misfortunes.

She drove towards town, then out again in the general direction of the moors, and almost without thinking came to where Drew's land was situated. She left the car and walked through the meadow and stood at the top of the hill and looked down. This, then, would be the new outlook for as long as she lived in her parents' house. Was Drew really as mercenary as Eric had suggested? Had he truly bought this land with an eye to re-selling a piece of it to her father at a profit? Was this really the sort of thing he did?

She tried not to believe it of him, but it certainly seemed an odd coincidence. And how was she going to feel living next door to Drew and Stephanie? She felt caught in a trap. She couldn't go back on her word now about helping to supervise the house-building. When the houses were completed and Drew was married she could, of course, find a flat in town for herself, but that would hurt her parents dreadfully. Whatever she did she was not going to be able to avoid contact with Drew at some time or other.

She sighed heavily. She supposed this was typical of a person in love. One minute thrilled at the idea of seeing the one you loved, the next shrinking from the idea of close contact with him. She started down the hill. What good had she done driving out here? Even if what Eric had said about Drew was true, it didn't really change anything. She wouldn't tell her parents what Eric had said, of course. And she still loved Drew She only felt sad and disappointed in him. Perhaps it *would* serve to help her put him out of her heart. If he were all set to marry Stephanie she would have to Clearly he was not the remotest bit in love with herself. If he were she would know about it.

Miserably, she churned things over and over again in her mind until hunger drove her back to her car and home. She would just have to grin and bear it. At any rate, bear it and try to be reasonably cheerful about things for her parents' sake.

She was home in time for lunch, after all, and had to

explain that she had changed her mind about going out to a meal with Eric. During the afternoon, encouraged by her mother, she set about designing a house for them, making copy after copy as her mother made first one suggestion, then another, and changed her mind so often they arrived back at the ideas first thought of. Cloak-rooms both at the front of the house and the back. A utility room where ironing and dressmaking could be done, a huge linen cupboard upstairs, large fitted ward-robes in each bedroom and a big boxroom also contain-ing cupboards.

Richard laughed, 'It doesn't matter how many cup-boards you have, you know, they'll all be full of some-thing or other in less than no time.'

'Well, if they're all full that proves they'll all be needed,' Helen retorted.

'Too many cupboards only encourage hoarding,' he insisted mildly.

'Nonsense,' returned his wife. 'What about all the clutter in the garage and shed, not to mention the cellar?'

'Which proves that I need somewhere to keep *my* belongings, too. So what about a study—all my very own? There's never been space in this house.'

Melanie was only half listening to this light-hearted exchange. She was wondering if, as Drew had suggested twin houses, whether similar requirements would suit him, too. She refused to think about Stephanie.

It seemed odd to look out from her bedroom window the next day and not see the two caravans there. Melanie wondered when they would see Drew again. Naturally enough most of the talk at home during the following days was of the new house. Drew rang up Richard after a few days had elapsed and said he had had an agreement drawn up about the land and planning permission had been applied for.

'He's coming over on Friday evening to talk to you about things,' Richard said to Melanie. 'He says there's no need to wait until everything's settled.'

Melanie's heart gave an uncontrollable lurch. 'No, I—suppose not. By the way, Father, were you happy about the price Drew asked for our building plot?'

'Good heavens, yes. It was very reasonable.'

'So you wouldn't say he made a profit?'

Richard frowned. 'How should I know? What on earth— Don't tell me you took any notice of what Eric said?'

Melanie lowered her gaze. 'Well, it is feasible when you come to think of it. And Drew didn't deny it when Eric said he had been doing this kind of thing—buying up land and selling at a profit.'

'And what's wrong with that?'

'But don't you think it's rather awful to take advantage of his position—his knowledge that people will be wanting building plots?'

Richard stared at her. 'You mean his knowledge— or rather his judgement—on where motorways are liable to run?'

'Yes.'

Her father shook his head. 'I don't think Drew would take unfair advantage of anybody. But, whichever way it is, he has solved our problem, hasn't he?'

'I suppose so.'

But still in her heart, Melanie did not feel happy about things, and determined that the next time she saw Drew she would ask him straight out whether he really had bought that land hoping to sell some of it.

When he arrived on Friday in time for dinner, Melanie was rather appalled to learn that he had been invited to stay the week-end. But resolutely she told herself that she would just simply have to get accustomed to being in his company.

She showed him the plan she had drawn of the ground and upper floor of her parents' house.

He studied them for a minute or two, then said, 'Yes,

these are good. Very good. Of course it's the fashion or whatever not to have either cellars or attics these days, but don't you think an attic—say with dormer windows —is a very useful thing to have? Lofts are a fearful waste of space and very inaccessible, and I think two and a half floors, as it were, would make the houses look better. Don't you agree? Like this.'

He drew rapid sketches of the exterior of the two different kinds of houses, and Melanie had to admit that the slightly taller houses with the upper dormer windows did look better.

' They'll be slightly more expensive to build, of course,' she said. ' But if that's the way you want yours and you'd like matching houses—'

He glanced at her sharply. ' You appear to have a very poor opinion of me. It's not only what *I* want that matters. We'll have to see what your mother and father think.'

Melanie felt suitably crushed, but felt sure that both her parents would agree with Drew about the two and a half storeys, as indeed they did.

' An attic with access by stairs instead of a loft ladder should solve even your storage problems,' Richard said teasingly to his wife.

' Then that's settled?' said Drew.

' There's only one problem with a pair of houses like this,' Melanie mused.

' Yes?' queried Drew.

' You may need a bigger house than we do.'

Drew picked up Melanie's plan of her parents' house. It would be a larger one than Hillrise, her mind ran on, but would one similar be large enough for what Eric had termed ' Drew's extravagant tastes '?

' One can have two houses which look almost identical from the outside, or from the front, at any rate,' he said, ' but the inside layout can be quite different. The inside can be divided into as many rooms of any size you want to suit individual requirements. Or more can be added on to the back and still keep frontal uniformity. Naturally, your mother has also had a hand in this design?'

Melanie nodded. 'It's the kind of house she has always wanted at heart—plenty of moderate sized rooms for different purposes. Hillrise was the only house they could find in the area at the time they wanted one. But would you like to see my suggested layout for *your* house?'

'Why, yes, I would—very much.'

The two *were* different inside. Melanie herself liked large rooms, and she guessed Drew would, too, though she had not a clue to what Stephanie would like. For Drew, Melanie had kept the domestic area of the house to a minimum. She had planned a kitchen which was labour-saving and in which all household chores would be done, including ironing, a job the modern housewife with a career cuts to a minimum. Her mother still clung to linen and cotton for sheets, tablecloths and curtains, whereas Melanie herself would make use of materials like nylon, fibreglass and crimplene. In her view a utility room on the ground floor took up unnecessary space. She would have one upstairs and dispense with a boxroom. She had designed an L-shaped dining room with a reception area, ideal either for entertaining or when a family was alone, and she had also provided for a larger sitting room. There was also a fair-sized room which could be used as a library or study.

Drew looked at the plan for a very long time. At last, she asked with misgivings: 'Well, what do you think?'

He started as if his thoughts had been far away. 'It's —great. Couldn't be better. I'll take both these plans and give them to an architect/surveyor to draw them up professionally and get them submitted to the local council for approval.'

For the rest of the evening the talk was of building materials, architect's plans, sizes and kinds of windows and doors. Melanie was fascinated, and lost in admiration at Drew's knowledge on these subjects.

'We can start ordering building materials right away,' he said. 'It takes time. Sometimes certain materials are in short supply and there are delays in deliveries. We shall need a watertight hut in which to store bags of cement and so on. In fact two huts. One as a shelter in case of heavy showers and where the men can make tea. We shall also have to search around for self-employed bricklayers. Doing it this way you save an enormous amount of money.'

'Providing you know something about the business— which you appear to,' said Richard. 'But how is it you *do* know so much about it?'

'I'm interested,' Drew answered. 'And I have here a book called *Fowler's Building Manual*. It tells you how many bricks you need per square foot, how many bags of cement per thousand bricks, roughly how many bricks an experienced bricklayer can lay in one hour— all kinds of things. Besides which there are all kinds of building regulations to which you have to comply with regard to material used. This, combined with the knowledge of the people you employ—it's dead easy.'

'To you, maybe, but it wouldn't be to me,' declared Richard.

'One of the main things, I gather, from people I know who have built their houses in this way, is to watch out that the men don't run short of the various materials. And that's where Melanie will probably be useful.'

'You mean as a sort of errand girl?' asked Melanie.

Drew nodded. 'I think we'd have to buy a little motorised truck. They're very useful for transporting the odd emergency bag of cement, piping—all kinds of little things one might overlook or run short of.'

'There are difficulties when the different workmen overlap, too, aren't there?' queried Melanie. 'Such as the plasterers and electricians, the painters and carpenters.'

'That's where we shall score building the two houses roughly at the same time. Yours will have priority, of course, but if they're stuck with one they can work on the other.'

'It really does sound as simple as A.B.C.,' Helen said, then added: 'But I don't know what we'd have done without you.'

To Melanie it seemed almost incredible that he should be taking all this trouble to help them. She thought wryly that Eric would have an answer. But watching Drew's face as he talked she knew she would forgive him whatever his motives. It was only when she remembered the existence of Stephanie that despair filled her heart.

Melanie saw Drew briefly at breakfast the following morning, then not again until she and her father arrived home about six o'clock after a busy day at the shop. Drew, it appeared, had had a busy day, too, seeking out bricklaying teams, locating builders' suppliers and plant hire people who would be ready to dig out the foundations when required. He had also taken Helen out to lunch.

'I was wondering,' he said to Melanie, 'whether you feel equal to coming out to dinner—and maybe dancing —unless you're too tired after your busy day.'

What about Stephanie? The question sprang into her mind immediately, but just in time she stopped herself giving utterance to it. If Drew did not think there would be any harm done, why should she? She felt suddenly reckless.

She smiled, 'Just give me half an hour to bath and change and I'll be right with you.'

'Good,' he said on a note of surprise. 'But take your time. I took a chance and booked a table for two.'

Her eyebrows arched. 'Oh, you did? And what would you have done if I'd already had a date?'

'In that case I would have taken my medicine and

simply cancelled the booking.'

Melanie went upstairs feeling as thrilled and excited as a schoolgirl going out on her first important date. She did not care about Stephanie. She did not care about anyone. She was spending a whole evening with Drew.

She took off her dress and lay on the bed with her eyes closed for a few minutes' relaxation and sweet contemplation. Before her vision floated a picture of herself dancing in Drew's arms, not the modern type of just swinging to the beat, but real ballroom dancing where you rested your hand on the man's shoulder, your other in his, and his left arm about your waist. Vaguely, at first, there were other couples dancing, then they were alone, and the next moment Drew had bent his head and his lips were on hers. For a brief spell it was bliss, then the vision was shattered by her mother calling her name and she realised she had fallen asleep for a moment or two.

' Have you been in the bathroom, Melanie?'

' No, Mother, not yet.'

' Well, do so soon, darling, will you? And let me know when you've finished.'

Melanie flung on a dressing gown and, her feeling of effervescence returning, hurried along to the bathroom. Back in her room it took a little time to decide what to wear. Did one dress up or dress down for a man like Drew? In the end she decided to dress to please herself and hoped also to please him. As she felt in a gay, exciting mood she dressed accordingly and wore a particularly glamorous culotte dress in a bold gold leaf pattern on white, the bodice cut low and the legs wide.

He was waiting in the hall when she descended the stairs, and she was relieved to see that he was wearing a dinner jacket. If he had not been she might have felt overdressed. She had the satisfaction of seeing his eyes widen when he caught sight of her.

He bowed. ' Well, well, I had no idea I was taking

out a duchess!'

'If it's too elaborate—' she began.

'On the contrary, I'm flattered. Or did you dress entirely to please yourself?'

'I dressed according to the way I was feeling—and hoped you would like it.'

He smiled. 'A very good reason—and I *do* like it. I'm glad I took the precaution of bringing a dinner jacket. If you're ready, we'll go, shall we?'

They called out goodbye to Richard and Helen and went out. Melanie thought Drew looked quite handsome and distinguished in his dinner jacket and was pleased that she had chosen to dress up. Some of her friends took a delight in dressing down, wearing the oddest assortment of clothes sometimes, but Melanie had a preference for dressing with a dash, and privately she liked a man to dress well, too.

Drew drove out to a country club Melanie knew quite well. It was rather expensive, but both the food and the service were good and so was the music of the three-piece dance orchestra. Whether by accident or design Drew had booked a table for two in an ideal situation, not too near the orchestra yet not too far away and fairly close to the dancing area. There was a small lamp on each table which shed a most flattering glow. Melanie had never felt happier.

'You're looking very beautiful tonight, Melanie,' Drew said unexpectedly.

Melanie felt a mixture of shyness and pleasure. 'Oh, Drew—'

He held out his hand. 'At the risk of the soup getting cold, let's dance, shall we?'

Melanie complied at once. The soup could go stone cold as far as she was concerned. She was not the least interested in food. With a feeling of inner excitement she slid into Drew's arms in time to the music. As she might have expected he was a good dancer, and she was glad that when she was a teenager she had learned this kind of dancing.

He spoke very little as he led her first into simple, ordinary steps, then gradually went into more intricate ones. Melanie felt she could go on dancing with him for ever. She had never felt so sublimely happy in her whole life.

'That was very nice, Melanie,' he said in a surprised tone when the dance was over.

'Why do you sound so surprised?' she asked lightly.

'You're a continual surprise to me,' he answered.

'Oh? In what way?'

'The number of things you can do exceptionally well.'

'I'm flattered.'

'Not flattery, the truth. Did you make the dress you're wearing?'

'Does it look home-made?'

'Of course not. I only ask because I know you do make your own clothes, and because it looks so good it's hard to believe that you *did* make it. Most women can do some of these kind of things moderately well and perhaps excel in one particular hobby or profession, but very few women excel in as many things as you do.' He smiled teasingly across the table.

Still in her rosy haze of happiness, Melanie returned his smile. 'So many compliments, just because I play the piano and do a little dressmaking?'

'*And* designing and helping to run a business as well as being a very good dancer. And as to the latter, I'm speaking from painful experience. Your mother tells me you can cook, too,' he added for good measure.

'My mother is prejudiced,' Melanie answered modestly, but she was pleased beyond measure at his high opinion of her few accomplishments.

He was the perfect companion. A good dancer, a good conversationalist, extremely knowledgeable about food and drink. If she was talented, he was even more so.

Once or twice thoughts of Stephanie crept into her mind and she toyed with the idea of asking him straight out whether he really were engaged to the girl, but she simply couldn't. It would sound dreadful. And so she dismissed Stephanie from her mind so firmly that before the evening was half over she had forgotten her existence completely. Melanie had never enjoyed an evening so much in her whole life. With each dance Drew became more and more affectionate, his arm encircling her waist more tightly, his right hand caressing hers. When the lights were lowered for waltzes she rested her head on his shoulder, quite uncaring about anything except that here she was in Drew's arms.

When they were not dancing they sat at their table drinking champagne and talking on all manner of subjects.

'Melanie—' mused Drew, 'if you—had a house, say, if you were married, what kind of life would you want to lead? Would you want to continue with your job in your father's business or would you stay at home and serve on committees—things like that?'

Melanie gazed dreamily into the far corner of the room. 'I think on the whole I'd be a home-lover. If—the man I married had a good enough job without the necessity of my having to earn money too, I'd prefer to stay at home. I'd want the home to be properly run, the garden to look as though it were cared for, my husband to be looked after well. I'd want our home to be a place of leisure, and how can it be when both husband and wife are rushing home at six, then starting to cook and having every week-end crowded out with odd jobs saved up from Monday to Saturday.'

Drew smiled, 'Lucky the man! But supposing you had enough money to be able to afford a daily woman, or a daily woman and a housekeeper as well as a regular gardener. What then?'

She thought for a moment. 'Speaking absolutely

personally I think I'd still want to be at home to look after things. I'd rather pay out less money in wages for domestic help. And I'd like to do some of the gardening, too.'

'Wouldn't you be lonely or even bored at home all day? The novelty of being at home all the time might wear off. And even if you had a family, wouldn't your outlook gradually become narrow over the years?'

'I'd certainly agree that it's something to watch. But I think there's a great need in society for women with a little time to spare. And still speaking for myself, I have my music. If a family came along I imagine they'd be a full-time job, and if after they grew up I found myself getting out of touch with life outside or bored, then I'd go out and find myself a job. But I still maintain that if a person doesn't have to work to earn a living, men or women, there's a crying need for their services in work for which there's no payment.'

'You mean voluntary work?'

She nodded. 'For instance there's the hospital car service for those who can drive—taking patients for physiotherapy and back home again, there's work with the Red Cross—'

Drew grimaced. 'I *have* heard married men complain that their wives are on so many committees they're hardly ever at home—worse than them being out at work.'

'So have I. Still, it's up to every married couple to work things out for themselves. It's wrong for either partner in my opinion to let work or hobbies come before each other.'

'The old give and take on both sides?'

'Of course. How else can marriage work? But let me put a question to *you*. If you were married would you like your wife to pursue a career, that is, go out to work, or would you rather think of her as being at home?'

Now, Drew's gaze became dreamy. 'I'd want her to do just whatever made her happy. Even though I can earn enough for both of us and to keep the house going, if she had a career and wanted to pursue it, then that would be fine by me.'

It was Melanie's turn to smile. 'Lucky woman! But your personal preference, Drew?'

'It would be that at any time during the day I could picture her at home, and on fine days, in the garden.'

'Ah, the old-fashioned type.'

'If that's what you like to call me. But then so are you, aren't you? Of course there are exceptions. Sometimes professional people like doctors, teachers and lawyers marry. Sometimes they are partners or colleagues and like that kind of life. It's meat and drink to them. Besides, not all women go out to work for financial reasons. They do it because their career is interesting, or useful to the community, or because they like to be among a lot of people.'

Melanie smiled at him. 'You're the most reasonable and understanding man I know.'

His brows arched. 'Much of that kind of flattery, young lady, and—well, you'd better watch out!'

'Watch out for what?' she asked teasingly.

He rose to his feet and held out his hand to her. 'Come along, let's dance.'

It was madness, she knew, but they danced almost cheek to cheek and for the rest of the evening behaved like a couple in love, holding hands coming from the dancing area, teasing each other, finding out about each other and completely enjoying one another's company. It was not until they arrived home that feelings of guilt on Stephanie's account began to impinge themselves on Melanie's consciousness. And yet, she argued, surely Drew would not behave as he had towards herself if he were really engaged. Or had she read too much into what was probably no more than a man having a mild flirtation with a girl he had taken out for an evening? He was not to know how she felt about him. At all events the evening was over now.

He drew up outside the house and Melanie automatically opened the car door to get out.

' Wait a moment, Melanie—'

But Melanie was already half out of the car, and when she looked back he was out, too.

' The front door won't be locked,' she said as they walked the few steps towards the house.

Suddenly she felt different, as if she had now come down from the high mountain to the reality below. But all at once as she was reaching out her hand to open the door Drew caught hold of her arm and swung her round to face him.

The next moment she was caught up in his arms and his lips were pressed down hard on hers.

CHAPTER VI

For a few blissful moments Melanie felt suspended on a cloud of purest joy. The whole universe seemed to stand still, and the moments of time were as eternity. Then as realisation came to her she stiffened and pushed against him.

'Drew, how could you? Let me go—please!'

He did so abruptly, and she hurried blindly into the house, pausing only long enough to note that apart from the hall the downstairs rooms were in darkness, before running straight upstairs.

You fool, she told herself breathlessly when she reached her room. *Why couldn't you have passed it off lightly?*

What would he think of her? Tears of hopelessness and frustration started into her eyes. The kiss had meant nothing to him, she was sure of it, and she did not want kisses without love from Drew. She simply could not take it. And if he had loved her he would have said so. She knew that she had probably spoilt the whole evening for both of them, but she simply could not help it. She knew also that, as he was a guest in her parents' house, she had been unforgivably rude to him, but she could not help that either. She would go downstairs and put out the light and lock the door later. She could not face him again tonight now. It would be bad enough in the morning.

She undressed, alert for any sound that would tell her Drew was coming upstairs to his room, but for a very long time there was no sound. Then, just as she was wondering whether or not she ought to go down, there came a quiet knock on her door. She opened it to see Drew standing there.

'I've locked the door and put out the light,' he told her in a cool, detached tone of voice. Then he added as he half turned to go to his room, ' Good night, Melanie, and—I'm sorry about what happened.'

' Thank you and—I'm sorry, too. Good night, Drew.'

Still with feelings of guilt about her behaviour Melanie slipped between the sheets. While they had been dancing it had been easy to keep up a pretence, to delude herself about him, but once outside, reality had set in. If only he had not kissed her. If only there was no Stephanie!

At breakfast the next morning Drew appeared to be his normal self, but Melanie could not help noticing that he addressed very few remarks directly to herself. Even when, naturally enough, Helen asked if they had enjoyed themselves the previous evening he answered briefly :

' You'd better ask Melanie that question.'

Melanie gave him a swift glance, but he kept his gaze on his plate. Helen looked at Melanie enquiringly.

' But of course we enjoyed it, Mother. Did you think we wouldn't?'

Helen shook her head. ' Not for a moment, dear. As a matter of fact I heard you come in—and somebody ran straight upstairs.'

Melanie closed her eyes momentarily. There were time when her mother was unwittingly tactless. But Drew saved her having to think of a suitable reply.

' I'm afraid I have to push off right after breakfast, Mrs Lawrence.'

' Oh, must you? We were hoping you'd stay until Monday morning. Couldn't you persuade him, Melanie?'

' I'll do my best, Mother, but you know Drew. Once he's made up his mind on anything—'

Drew—deliberately, it seemed to Melanie—did not even glance at her. He began to talk to her father about some aspect of the building programme.

Her mother had started to clear away when the telephone rang. Richard went to answer it and Helen followed a moment later with a pile of dishes.

' Melanie—' Drew said as Melanie prepared to do the

same, 'can I have a word with you?'

She turned. 'If—it's about last night, Drew, I'm sorry. It was very silly of me, I realise that now. After all, what's a kiss after an evening out? I don't know what possessed me. It was not only silly, it was very rude of me to dash away like that. You might have wanted a drink or something.'

She spoke swiftly as if to forestall anything he might think or say.

He looked at her for a moment, then said stiffly: 'I see. Well, I'm glad you're not too offended at any rate. As to apologies, there are none needed from you. It was a pleasant evening out, and it is I who owe you apologies as well as thanks.'

But there was something wrong, somehow. His manner was stilted and she felt a barrier between them.

'Melanie!' It was her father's voice from the hall. 'Eric is on the phone for you. Can you come?'

'Coming, Father!'

She hesitated, still feeling troubled, but her father came into the room and so she went out.

Her mind still with Drew she picked up the receiver. 'Hello, Eric—'

'Melanie!' came his bright voice. 'How are you?'

'Fine—and you?'

'Missing you. Are you free today?'

'Yes, I—I think so.' She did not really want to see him, but what else could she say? Drew was leaving this morning, and in any case—

'Good. I'll call for you about three and we'll go out to tea somewhere. All right?'

She agreed, only half concentrating. If only she hadn't been so silly last night. At least she and Drew might have still been friends. Instead of which his manner had considerably cooled towards her.

When she went back into the dining room he was no longer there and she assumed that he had gone to his room to pack. She drifted into the kitchen to help her mother, who immediately began talking.

'I wonder why Drew is going so soon. Did anything happen between you last night?'

'What on earth do you mean, Mother?' Melanie picked up the teacloth and prayed that her mother would not probe too far. 'We had a thoroughly enjoyable evening.'

'I just thought it odd—your dashing straight upstairs like that. And odder still that he should be pushing off so soon today. We quite thought he was staying until later, at least.'

'Well, I'm sure he isn't leaving on my account, Mother.'

But she wasn't really as sure as all that. In dramatic terms she had repulsed him last night. And no man likes that.

Half an hour later Drew was downstairs, luggage in hand and saying his goodbyes and thanks.

'I'll be in touch,' he said. 'And when the building starts proper I shall have my caravan on the site and take my holiday. It will be up to Melanie to decide when she takes hers. Goodbye, all.'

His glance brushed over Melanie lightly. Doubtless he was greatly regretting becoming even remotely romantic yesterday evening, she thought miserably. She sighed heavily and went indoors. How was she going to face the future without Drew's love? Life was going to be impossible. Once her parents' house was built she must think of something. Have a flat in town. Save some money and travel. Or study music more seriously and become a professional. That way, she might travel the country or even tour Europe. Somehow she would have to get Drew out of her system.

She had almost forgotten about Eric until he arrived. Her parents had gone to visit friends, and she was playing the piano, a part of her mind still occupied with thoughts of Drew. She started violently as Eric's head came round the door of the room.

'Hope you didn't mind my coming in,' he said. 'I rang the bell, but obviously you didn't hear—and I could hear you playing.'

She apologised, 'Do you mind waiting while I change? I meant to be ready, but once I start playing—'

'I don't mind waiting,' he told her, 'though you look all right to me as you are.'

All the same she went upstairs to change. She could not help noticing that Eric showed not the slightest interest in her kind of music, and though the question of marriage to him did not arise, she thought suddenly how awful it would be to be married to someone who did not care for music and was bored by her playing.

She changed, and Eric drove through town and made for the moors. He was a great talker, and normally Melanie appreciated conversation, but today she was preoccupied with thoughts of her own, all centred around Drew.

At last Eric said, 'You're very quiet today. Anything wrong?'

'No, no, of course not.'

'All going well with regard to the new house?'

She felt herself stiffen. 'Yes, very well, thank you. And I think I should tell you that Drew asked a very reasonable price for the land he sold to Father.'

Eric shrugged. 'Oh, I daresay. But that doesn't alter the fact that he makes a profit on these deals. I'm not blaming him, don't get me wrong. But I've been finding out things about Drew Hamilton.'

'Really?' Melanie said icily.

'Hm-m. He's worth quite a bit of money. He doesn't really have to work.'

'Very interesting!'

Eric gave her a swift glance. 'You sound as though you don't believe me. I got it from the one person who should know. Stephanie.'

'I didn't know you knew her,' Melanie returned swiftly.

'Oh, I bumped into her one day. Quite by chance.'

'How?—if she lives in the Lake District?' Melanie demanded.

'She was in Chesterfield. She'd come to see Drew, but he wasn't around.'

'Didn't he know she was coming?'

Eric gave her a sidelong glance, then laughed. 'How should I know? Maybe he did.'

'So you "bumped into Stephanie" and proceeded to gossip about Drew,' Melanie said tartly.

Eric was no longer laughing. There was a short silence, then he said huffily: 'What's biting you, Melanie? It was Stephanie who volunteered the info, I didn't pump her. As a matter of fact, it was the boot on the other foot. She was asking *me* about *you*—wondered where you fitted in with Drew.'

'And what did you tell her?'

'I told her she needn't worry on that score. Was I right?'

'Perfectly. He's helping us to build our house, and after that I don't expect to see much of him at all.'

'But your folks and he will be neighbours, won't they?'

'Yes, but I may get myself a flat in town or even travel.'

'Travel?' he echoed. 'What doing?'

'I—I'm not sure yet.'

She did not want to talk to him about her—as yet— only half-formed ideas. They were too closely allied to her heartache on Drew's account. So she said no more, and decided to herself that this was the very last time she would accept an invitation out from Eric.

He was not so easily put off, however. Out of courtesy she felt obliged to ask him in to supper when they arrived home, and when he left he asked when he could see her again.

She shook her head. ' Sorry, Eric, but I shall be too busy during the coming months. It's—going to be a sort of race against time to get the new house built before the bulldozers start ploughing through Hillrise.'

' But what on earth are *you* going to do, for goodness' sake?'

She tried to explain and could readily understand the look of amusement and incredulity which this brought to his face.

' But it's ridiculous!' he said.

' Ridiculous or not, I'm going to do it. Father doesn't want to and so—'

' You're playing the " son " again.'

' That's right,' Melanie said tersely.

Eric shrugged. ' Oh, well, I'll drop by and see how you're getting along one of these days. O.K.?'

' Of course.'

There was little else she could say. She did not want to be rude to him or rebuff him outright, but she really would rather not see him again. At one period of their relationship it did seem that he was becoming fond of her, but she felt certain this had passed, and for her part she liked him less each time she saw him. He had always something carping to say about Drew.

As was anticipated the plans for Drew's house were passed before those of Melanie's parents as they had been ready to be submitted first. Drew wasted no time in ordering building materials to be delivered to the site and two huts to be erected. Melanie went out there with him one early closing day. He had telephoned previously to arrange the visit, and she had been in a fever of inner excitement and apprehension at the thought of seeing him again. But her apprehension, at any rate, was unfounded. Drew's manner showed not the slightest sign of the restraint or coolness she had half anticipated.

He was perfectly friendly, perfectly polite and perfectly natural. At first Melanie was relieved and delighted, but gradually an odd sense of dissatisfaction and disappointment assailed her.

She was in love with him. She did not want him merely to be polite. She would rather he were angry with her. As it was, she sensed something wrong about their relationship. It was superficial. But was a real depth of friendship possible, feeling as she did about him?

'There you are, Melanie,' he said, when they arrived at the building site. 'Officially, these bricks and blocks, the sand and aggregate, and the bags of cement are for my house. But what it means in reality is that the moment your plans for the house are passed we can start right away without waiting for stuff to be delivered.'

'What about the foundations? Will there be much delay about the plant hire?'

He shook his head. 'What we *can* do is have the architect along to mark them out. And I've booked the plant hire and ready mixed concrete tentatively. They'll come at forty-eight hours' notice and do the foundations for both houses.'

'And what about the bricklaying team?'

'They expect to be finished the job they're on at the moment in about ten days' time. After that, we start paying them, even if they have to stand by for a few days. I thought it best, otherwise they might start on another job—and good bricklaying teams are hard to find.'

She gave him a look of gratitude. 'You're being awfully good and helpful, you know, Drew.'

'Nonsense. I'm getting my own house built at the same time—remember?'

'Drew—' she said suddenly, 'did you have in mind *at all* when you bought this land—my parents' probable requirements?'

He turned and looked at her. 'Why do you ask?'

She shrugged. 'It's—just something to which I'd like an answer.'

'If you want the truth—yes, I did. But please don't ask me why because I'd rather not tell you.'

She wished she hadn't asked. It seemed Eric was right, after all. She had expected him to say no, naturally. Drew had bought the land with the idea, not only of building a house for himself, but with that of selling at least a part of it. Some people would not see anything wrong in that, but to Melanie it savoured of cashing in on the predicament of others, using his pre-knowledge of what was going to happen, and if he were in the habit of doing that—

She felt Drew's gaze fixed upon her. 'What's the trouble?' he asked.

She shook her head. 'Nothing.'

He strolled around the site examining the materials, going inside the huts, one of which contained bags of cement.

Melanie watched him. If he were guilty of sharp practice how could she be in love with him? Was it possible to love a person if his character was not according to your ideal? She felt confused. She did love him, there was no doubt whatever about that. But her disappointment in him was due to something else. She couldn't quite think what for a while, then at last it came to her. She had wanted him to say that he had offered her father the piece of land for her sake. She was seeking for signs, however small, for any regard he might have for her. One was rarely content, it seemed, just to love. One wanted to be loved in return.

Drew was coming back to her side. 'We're very fortunate indeed that it's the beginning of summer,' he said. 'All we shall need in the men's hut is a liquid gas thing for boiling a kettle. There'll be no heat required.'

'You seem to set great store by making the workmen

comfortable,' she told him. 'A shelter from the rain, the wherewithal to make tea—'

He gave a faint smile. 'It's not just philanthropy. If the men have somewhere to shelter from the rain they're more likely to wait until it stops. If there isn't, they'll pack up and go home. It's as simple as that.'

Melanie looked at him, a new kind of interest stirring within her. What kind of man was he, really? She realised with a sudden stab that she scarcely knew him. She had thought she did.

During the months of that summer she had plenty of time in which to study and speculate about the true nature and character of Drew, and though there were times when her heartache threatened to become more than she could bear, she loved him more with each day that passed.

The plans for the Lawrences' house were duly passed and the foundations of both houses laid. For the first few weeks Drew had very little time to spare from his job, but he was in constant touch with Melanie by telephone, made all arrangements with the bricklayers to start, and ordered the delivery of window frames and door frames. The building materials ordered ostensibly for Drew's house were used for the Lawrences' so as to afford as little delay as possible. Melanie would run over to the site during the day to make sure the men had all they wanted, and Drew would be there at the weekends. It seemed to Melanie that fantastic progress was made in a very short time.

'Ah, yes,' Drew said. 'It does seem that way at first. Some of these experienced workmen can lay a thousand bricks a day—with a labourer mixing the mortar and keeping the bricklayers supplied with bricks. The thing is not to let them run short of sand and cement, and that's where you come in. In another couple of weeks I shall have finished my contract for this particular stretch of motorway, then I shall take a few months off and bring my caravan here. You have to keep an eye on even the best of workers, and it will be even more necessary when the bricklayers start on my house and the interior work on yours begins.'

Melanie found it all both interesting and exciting. When she did not ring Drew, he rang her, asking for a report on how things were going and giving her advice. He was certainly a man of action and a great organiser. The more she saw of him the more she admired him.

She had almost forgotten the existence of both Eric and Stephanie when one day by some odd chance they arrived on the scene together. Drew had had a rough kind of road made to the site and only that morning had towed his caravan to the site.

Drew was standing bareheaded in the breeze, his shirt open at the neck, his sleeves rolled up and his arms akimbo as he cast a critical eye over the fitting of the frame of a large picture window. He made the most attractive figure of a man and Melanie experienced a longing for his love which was more than she could bear.

He turned at the approach of the two cars and walked across to open the door for Stephanie.

'Well, this is a surprise. I thought you were in Windermere? And how come you and Eric are in convoy?'

Stephanie kissed him on the cheek. 'One question at a time, please, darling. Actually, it's almost as much of a surprise to me. I only knew yesterday that my firm wanted me to come to their Sheffield branch for the summer. A sudden replacement required—someone ill —no one else would leave Windermere during the summer. Neither would I for a place like Sheffield, normally, but with you here—'

'You'll like the shops in Sheffield,' Drew told her in a teasing voice.

'And the answer to your second question,' Eric put in, having joined them, ' is that I came across Stephanie having had a puncture.'

'And like a good " knight of the road " you gallantly changed her wheel for her.'

Now Drew's tongue had an edge to it, Melanie noticed. Was he jealous of Eric? She did not think for a moment that he had any real cause, but jealousy was often unreasoning where love was concerned.

'Naturally,' Eric answered. 'She also wasn't sure of the way.'

'And you were.'

'This is my stamping ground, remember? It's you who are the "foreigner".' Eric turned to Melanie. 'Well, and how's my girl? The building going according to plan?'

Melanie knew a moment's irritation at being called his girl, but she made no comment and invited him to come and look at the building. He showed only a perfunctory interest, however, except to enquire: 'And when is the building to start on Hamilton's house?'

'As soon as the bricklayers have finished on ours,' she told him.

'I see. And when is the happy day going to be?'

'What happy day?'

'Why, the wedding of Stephanie and Hamilton.'

'I'm sure I don't know,' Melanie answered stiffly.

Eric grinned, 'I think Stephanie made a very wise move, coming to work in Sheffield. You're a very attractive girl.'

'And what is that supposed to mean?' demanded Melanie, though she was perfectly well aware of what he was driving at.

Eric told her so. 'Don't be so naïve. She's jealous of you.'

'How do you know she is?'

'It's sticking out a mile.'

'Well, she needn't worry. Drew and I keep strictly to the work in hand.'

'Strictly?' queried Eric.

'I said strictly and I meant it, so will you please let the matter drop, Eric.'

'Sure.'

Stephanie and Drew were standing on what was to be their house. As yet only the foundations were laid, but Drew was pointing out where the various rooms would be. The next moment, Stephanie's arm linked in his, they were strolling down to the river. Melanie watched them miserably. So Stephanie was going to be in Sheffield for the summer—a mere seventeen miles away. This was a fact, whatever her motive.

The weather was extremely favourable for building work. For weeks there was scarcely more than a few light showers. By working overtime, the bricklayers reached the roof of the Lawrences' house in just over a month.

'It's quite fantastic!' Melanie exclaimed to Drew as he surveyed what almost looked like a completed house. 'I can hardly credit the stories I've heard of it taking anything from six months to a year to build a house.'

Drew laughed. 'They'll be true, I assure you. You have no idea—and I hope you won't experience it on this job—the delays that can happen in house-building. But apart from that, the brickwork is really only a small part of a building, important as it may be and look. It's the interior and finishing off that takes time. There are the dividing walls, the plumbing, the ceilings, skirting, doors to be fitted, the kitchen and bathroom, not to mention all the painting inside and out.'

'Heavens, the way you put it, it's a wonder any house gets completed *within* a year ever!'

He patted her shoulder. 'Don't worry. This one will be, if I have to do some of the work myself.'

Melanie glanced at him curiously. 'Why, Drew?' she asked quietly.

His head came round sharply. 'What do you mean

—why?'

Melanie almost shrank under his hard scrutiny. 'I—I mean why should you do all this for—for us?'

'Why not?' he countered. 'Is it so difficult to believe that I'd do something to help someone unless I'm making a profit out of it?'

Melanie drew in a shocked breath as he stamped angrily away. Later she attempted to apologise.

'I'm sorry, Drew, but very few people *are* willing to do so much without a motive.'

He gave a swift, unsmiling shake of his head. 'Please say no more about it, Melanie.'

She turned unhappily away. Had she hurt his pride or—or did he really have some hidden motive not yet revealed?

He could not have given more attention to his own house than he did to the Lawrences'. He watched critically each stage of the operation. He eyed keenly the carpenter as he inserted the cross-beams for the ceilings and the roof, the joiner who hung the doors and the men who divided off the rooms. Melanie was continually amazed at his store of knowledge.

'Is there anything you can't do, Drew?' she asked him teasingly one day.

He darted a swift glance at her with his blue-grey eyes. 'Yes, any number of things. I can't make a woman—' He halted abruptly, and the stern lines of his face deterred her from any further questions.

She recalled something Eric had said about Drew. That he acted like a man who has something to hide. Did he *really* love Stephanie, or had there been a greater love in his life, one which had been disappointing? Perhaps Stephanie was a sort of second best. She didn't really seem Drew's type. Melanie thought ruefully that she herself would willingly be second best in Drew's life. Anything except this relationship she had at the moment. It was no kind of relationship at all. What he was doing he was doing for her parents.

As the work progressed, Melanie took her 'holiday' from the shop. She stayed at a small hotel as near to the building site as possible, and as work was now being done on both houses Melanie was kept quite busy on all kinds of errands to builders' suppliers, timber yards and hardware shops.

Not really surprisingly, unless specially arranged, the visits of Stephanie and Eric did not coincide again. As both had a job to do, most of their visits were confined to Saturdays and Sundays, and though the men did not work on Saturday afternoons and evenings, Drew and Melanie did. To push the work forward Drew decided to do the interior paintwork himself, and Melanie felt it only fair that she should help.

Melanie had never realised before how much paintwork there was in a house. There were door frames, architraves, window frames and sills and what seemed to be miles and miles of skirting, all of which needed two undercoats with rubs down with glasspaper in between to remove the harsh grains which the paint brought out. Melanie knew none of these things until Drew taught her.

'How on earth did you learn all this?' she asked him.

'From my father.'

It was the first time she had heard him mention his father. 'He—wasn't a professional painter?'

'No, he was an engineer, but he could turn his hand to most things, and what he did he did well.'

'Like you.'

He gave her a long look, as if he found it hard to believe she was being genuinely complimentary.

'If you say so. But if it's true of me, then it's doubly so of you. There are some people who do everything well—at least, everything they put their hands to— simply because they're intelligent and conscientious.'

Melanie made no comment for a moment or two. It was nice to be praised and thought well of by him, but—

'What about Stephanie?' she asked, following her train of thought.

'Stephanie?' He laughed. 'I think Stephanie does only one thing well.'

'And what's that?'

He gave a slow smile. 'Just being herself.'

Melanie turned away and applied her paint in fierce concentration. What greater compliment could a man pay to a woman? It reminded her of a very old saying: *Be good, sweet maid, and let who will be clever.* Drew thought she herself was talented. But what was the good of that?

A car was heard and Melanie looked through the window to see Stephanie arriving.

She turned to tell Drew. 'Shall I go and make some tea?'

'No, I'll go. You take a break. You look as if you need one.'

As soon as the weather had become warm enough to sit outside Drew had brought some canvas chairs and a garden table. Melanie greeted Stephanie and led her towards them.

'Drew has gone to make some tea,' she said. 'He won't be long.'

'Why didn't you make it?' Stephanie demanded unexpectedly.

Melanie looked at her in surprise. 'I did offer, but—'

'Poor Drew! I think it's too bad that he has all this extra work to do. He had planned to go abroad this summer.'

'I didn't know that,' Melanie said sharply.

'No, I don't suppose you did. Drew is like that. And don't tell him I told you. It *should* have been our honeymoon, but Drew felt so sorry for your parents, and once he's promised to help someone—which he's always doing—'

Melanie felt her cheeks growing pink. She was beginning to feel like a poor relation—a nuisance.

'I'm very sorry to hear all this, Stephanie. I had no idea. But we didn't *ask* Drew to do it, you know. He wanted to.'

'Oh, I daresay,' shrugged Stephanie. 'But from all accounts you and your parents were terribly eager.'

Melanie compressed her lips angrily. 'I think we'd better end this conversation. As to Drew helping us, *I* intend to help with the work on *your* house, you know.'

Stephanie gave a laugh of derision. 'Really? How kind of you. But don't think you'll make any impression on Drew. He's far too much in love with me to want any other woman—though he may not always show it.'

Melanie drew herself up angrily. 'Really, Stephanie! What an awful thing to say! I'm not trying to make any impression whatever on Drew, as you call it.'

'No? Well, here he comes. I agree with you—we'd better put an end to the conversation.'

Drew placed the tray on the table and asked Stephanie to pour out. Melanie leaned her head back on the canvas chair feeling absolutely mortified. So Stephanie thought she was helping with the work on the houses merely to try to attract Drew. Hadn't Drew told her that it had all been his own idea?

'Melanie—'

She opened her eyes to see Drew holding a cup of tea out to her. He eyed her critically.

'You know, you look ready for a rest. Why don't you take a few days off? A week-end, at least.'

'Yes, why don't you?' added Stephanie. 'I can come and give Drew a hand.'

'You?' laughed Drew.

'Yes, why not? Any fool can paint a few yards of skirting. There's nothing to it as far as I can judge.'

'There's more to it than you think,' Drew told her tersely. 'Besides, you'll ruin your nails.'

Drew obviously preferred her to be decorative rather than useful, Melanie thought dully.

'I should think you could do with a break, too,' she told him, mindful of what Stephanie had told her. 'I think I'll take next week-end off. I'll go home. You can have my room at the hotel, Stephanie, then you and Drew can spend the week-end together.'

'How lovely! Thank you,' Stephanie said with a mocking smile. 'And I'm sure you and Eric will be glad of a little time together, too.'

Melanie made no reply to this. What was the use? Stephanie went on talking, addressing most of her remarks to Drew, and Melanie drifted into a melancholy world of her own.

Quite suddenly Drew stood up. 'Sorry, Stephanie. Must get on. If you want to help, perhaps you wouldn't mind washing these tea-things. You've got to get your hand in some time.'

Melanie drove home the following Friday evening. By this time, Drew had had a temporary telephone installed in his caravan, and he promised to ring her if anything urgent happened.

'Not that it's likely to,' she said ruefully. 'In fact, now that we've got the phone you hardly need me.'

'Why do you say that?' he asked swiftly. 'Have you had enough?'

She shook her head. 'Not unless *you*'ve had enough of *me*.'

He gave her a hard stare. 'It's entirely up to you, Melanie. The work will go ahead quicker with your help, but if you're finding it too much—'

She shook her head swiftly. She would have given anything for him to say that *he* needed her. But what was the use? She really would have to stop reaching for the stars.

She had decided to take a long week-end at home and go through her personal things, tidy her drawers and so on in preparation for the time when she, along with her parents, would have to move out, and so had arranged to return to the hotel and building site on Monday morning.

Drew looked at her oddly as she prepared to set off. 'Have a nice week-end, Melanie. Relax—play the piano. You must have missed it.'

'I have, in a way.' She smiled suddenly. 'I'll bring it back with me. Maybe you can find room for it in your caravan.'

The severe lines of his face relaxed into a slow smile. 'Wish I could. Seems ages since I heard you play.' Then he cautioned, as if anxious now for her to be off, 'Drive carefully. See you Monday morning.'

She drove off, a mixture of feelings. How awfully nice he could be sometimes, and how wonderful it would be to be loved by him. She hovered between happiness and heartbreak. The feeling of joy and happiness that love always brings accompanied by the heartbreak of not being loved in return. Liking, concern, a certain admiration of one's gifts—these were not enough. Her need to mean something more to him was growing increasingly real and desperate with each day that passed.

Spring had now passed into summer, and it was a simply glorious evening. She had the advantage of driving towards the east which meant that the sun was behind her, showing the Derbyshire countryside in all its beauty and splendour—the wooded valleys and streams, the mountains and the rolling moors. It would break her heart ever to leave this part of the country, but unless she could do something about this love she had for Drew she would have to—for a little while, at least.

Feeling the need to compose herself and try to cull a little peace of mind from the countryside about her, Melanie ran her car into a parking space off the road. She sat at the wheel for a little while, then decided to take a walk. Why could one not be content with loving a person without wanting to be loved in return? It should be possible. She would have to make it so, otherwise she would never more have any peace of mind for as long as she lived. An exaggeration? Not the way she felt at the moment.

She climbed a stile and strode across the moor, trying to come to terms with the unhappy situation in which she had found herself. She would have to accept the fact that Drew was in love with someone else. She ought to be happy for his sake. She took a deep breath and decided to turn back. She would have to see the building project right through now, but after that—

She reached the stile again and felt a pang of loneliness as she saw, a little further along under the shelter of the grey stone wall, a pair of lovers in a close embrace. Neither looked up as she climbed the stile, and a sudden wild idea caused her to take another look at them. She drew a swift breath and dropped quickly on to the other side.

There was absolutely no doubt about it. The pair of ' lovers ' were Eric and Stephanie.

CHAPTER VII

Melanie crossed the road and walked swiftly to her car a few yards up the road further on. It was incredible. How *could* Stephanie when she was going to marry Drew? How *could* she? And Eric was equally to blame.

She started her car and continued on her journey. A short distance along on the opposite side of the road was another parking place, and a swift glance showed Eric's car standing there—a low red convertible. Her own was a dark blue. There were thousands like it. Neither Eric nor Stephanie could have noticed it, otherwise they would not have chosen that spot to—

She broke off her unpleasant thoughts worriedly. How awful for Drew to be marrying a woman who would behave in such a frivolous way. But suppose she and Eric were genuinely in love—had only just discovered it? That would make their behaviour a little less despicable, perhaps, but she could not think which would be worse for Drew. Either way would bring him unhappiness. She was convinced that neither Eric nor Stephanie had seen her. They had not moved a muscle. Melanie would not speak of it to either of them, she decided, and certainly not to Drew. If they were genuinely in love surely Stephanie would break with Drew during the next few days. Melanie told herself she would simply have to wait and see.

She arrived home in time for supper, and naturally enough her mother and father plied her with questions about the building progress.

'It's odd you should have chosen this week-end to come home,' her mother said. 'Your father and I were all set to come over and spend a whole day with you and Drew. We weren't able to come last Sunday, and we won't next Sunday either. Still, perhaps we can go, even so, if you want a rest from all that.'

Melanie shook her head swiftly. 'No, no, Mother, I shouldn't do that if I were you. Stephanie will be spending the week-end with Drew. She's—having my room at the hotel.'

'Oh,' Helen said in a disappointed voice. 'Is she really? Well, in that case—'

'Why don't you come over on the next half day closing?' suggested Melanie. 'We could have a picnic lunch if it's fine. And if not, we could have lunch at my hotel. What do you say, Father?'

They agreed to do this, then Helen asked curiously: 'Does Stephanie go over to the site a lot?'

'Fairly often—yes.'

'And Eric?'

'Sometimes.'

Helen eyed Melanie keenly. 'You know, you don't look too good. I hope you're not working too hard on that house.'

'No, of course I'm not, Mother. I'm enjoying it.' To change the subject Melanie turned to her father. 'How're things at the shop, Father? Still managing all right without me?'

He smiled at her. 'We're missing you—and I mean that. Quite frankly, I had no idea how much you did.'

Melanie was silent for a moment, thinking of her half-formed plan of going abroad. This was not the time to talk about her plans, she felt sure, but—

'Father—' she began slowly, 'do you think perhaps you ought to get another assistant? A secretary, maybe. We—shall be quite some time on this building project, and—'

'Oh no, Melanie, that isn't necessary. Peter is very good. Besides, I'd have the tiresome business later of telling the secretary she was redundant. And don't tell me I could advertise for someone part-time. I hate part-timers.'

Melanie frowned worriedly. How could she persuade him without telling him—and her mother—the whole truth, which she did not want to at this stage, even if it would be right to ever.

But oddly enough it was here that her mother came in. 'You know, Richard, I think Melanie is right. You ought to have someone. A secretary—or an assistant. Yes, that would be better—an assistant. Someone who could attend to the letters for you and then help where required in any of the departments.'

'A sort of "Melanie", you mean?'

Helen laughed. 'Well, she would hardly be that, would she? But you do need help—even when Melanie comes back. It's time you took life a little more easily, had more leisure. You should be able to leave early some days, take one off occasionally. Instead of that you're there attending to things after everyone else has gone home.'

Melanie was alerted. 'Are you, Father?'

He gave a slightly impatient gesture. 'Oh, sometimes. But your mother is exaggerating. It's only temporary until you come back, and it's nothing to what you're doing out at Curbar. Anyway, what *is* all this? The pair of you suddenly ganging up against me?'

'Not *against* you, Father. *For* you. I think Mother is right. Get a personal assistant, if you don't like the term secretary. I—I think *I* might want a little more time off, too, when I come back. I'd like to devote a little more time to my music, do more concert work.'

'There you are!' exclaimed Helen. 'And I think Melanie is quite right. She may not always be with us, you know, and the sooner you get used to the idea the better.'

'Helen, what are you driving at?' asked Richard a little exasperatedly.

Melanie herself was rather startled by her mother's

unexpected support and what seemed almost uncanny foresight, though of course she could have been referring to the time—almost certainly was—when Melanie would marry. Even so—

'Really, Richard, you should know perfectly well what I'm driving at. You don't suppose Melanie is going to stay single all her life just to act as your secretary-cum-assistant manager, do you? She might be getting married sooner than you think, and there are *some* men who don't like their wives to go out to work. Besides, you heard what she said. She wants more time for her music.'

Richard sighed. 'Very well. I can't stand out against the two of you any longer. I think I must be getting old. I'll start advertising for someone.'

'Good,' Helen said briskly. 'And if you take my advice, you'll look for someone in her thirties, not a young girl. Older women are often more adaptable, don't mind what they turn their hands to.'

'But Melanie's young—'

'Melanie is different.'

Melanie couldn't help noticing the subtle change in her mother. She was more firm, calm, more in command. Or could it be that Melanie and her father—particularly her father—had been wrong about her mother all these years? She looked at her father and thought he was indeed looking rather tired.

'Father, would you like me to come along to the shop tomorrow and lend a hand?'

It was her mother who answered. 'No, darling. You need a rest. You must be working very hard out there. What's the use of your coming home for a week-end off if you're going to work all day tomorrow at the shop? Your father can rest up on Sunday.'

'Yes, of course,' Richard said. 'I wouldn't dream of letting you come, Melanie—thanks all the same.'

Melanie played the piano for a while, then went to

bed. She thought of Drew and of Stephanie and Eric and worried a little, but she was so mentally exhausted, she fell asleep quite quickly and did not waken the next morning until almost nine when her mother entered with her breakfast.

'Mother, you shouldn't have done this!'

Helen smiled, 'Shouldn't I? Why not?'

'Well, it—it doesn't seem right.'

'It's perfectly right. You and your father between you have taken charge of me quite long enough. Now it's my turn, so get on with your breakfast and I'll have a cup of tea with you.'

She brought up a chair. Melanie poured out the tea and eyed her mother with a mixture of interest and amusement.

'And what has brought about this sudden change in you, Mother?'

Helen sipped her tea. 'It's not as sudden as you might think. Your father has protected me—or tried to —from the hard knocks of life ever since we've been married, and he's brought you up to do the same. Don't think I haven't been aware of it.'

This was truly astonishing. 'But, Mother, you've always taken things so badly, that's why—'

'It was your dear, silly father. He always hated to see me cry, but that was just my way of expressing things. I was never brought up to "keep up a stiff upper lip", but to express my feelings naturally.'

'But why are you telling me this now? Why did you let Father—and me—go on protecting you?'

'I don't know. It was just one of those things. I'd got used to it, I suppose. Your father accepted troubles philosophically. I didn't. As to why I'm telling you this now—well, to be honest, one or two things Drew said to me went home. I'm not nearly as fragile or weak as you and your father seem to think. Besides, I'd noticed you were beginning to rebel a little. You were, weren't you?'

Melanie smiled slightly. 'Perhaps. It was nice of you to tell me, anyway, Mother. But what did Drew say to you?'

But Helen shook her head. 'Oh, just little things. But what about you? You looked more than tired last night. There's something wrong, isn't there?'

Melanie spread a piece of toast in silence. It was a great temptation to pour out everything, but what good would it do except to relieve her own pent-up emotions? But perhaps this *was* the time to speak openly about some of her plans.

'There *are* one or two things I'd like to tell you, Mother, and I'll leave it to you to tell Father. I've been thinking that when we move into the new house I'd like to have a flat in town, if you don't mind.'

Helen's blue eyes widened. 'A flat in town—in Chesterfield? But why? Oh, I know lots of girls do, it's the fashion now, I daresay, but—but you have complete freedom at home.'

'Yes, I know, Mother, but—well, Curbar is a longer way out and so many of my friends live here—'

'But it will be the same for your father and me—'

Melanie gave an inaudible sigh. 'Please, Mother, I must. I need to. Don't make it difficult. What I said last night was true. I do want to give more time to my music.'

'And I agree with that. I think you should. But you can practise at home as much as you like. You always have been able to.'

'I know that, but I—'

She broke off, reluctant to say what her real reason was for wanting a flat. Why? Because she was afraid her mother might try some embarrassing match-making efforts?

'I'm—thinking I might gradually become a professional pianist, Mother, travel around a bit, even go abroad.'

Helen eyed her in thoughtful silence for a minute or two. Then she said quietly: ' How long has all this been going through your mind?'

' Oh—lately, that's all.'

' Since you met Drew Hamilton, in fact.'

Melanie gave her mother a startled look. ' Well, he —he did once ask me why I hadn't made the piano my profession, but—'

' You're in love with him, aren't you?'

Melanie drew in a swift breath and started to say something, but tears she could not stop filled her eyes. She shook her head swiftly. ' Please, Mother, I don't want to talk about it.'

' Darling—' Helen covered her daughter's hand, ' it might be better if you *do* talk about it. Is that why you don't want to live in the new house—because Drew will be our next-door neighbour?'

Melanie nodded. ' I—I simply couldn't bear it, Mother, especially when he's married to Stephanie.'

' But are you sure he's going to be?'

' Yes. In fact Stephanie told me only the other day that this time Drew is taking off should have been their honeymoon.'

Helen frowned and shook her head. ' But Drew has never said anything about getting married, and she doesn't look his type in the least.'

' It's no *use*, Mother. Why else would he be having a house like that built? And why else does Stephanie come all the way from the Lake District to see him? In fact, Mother, she's working in Sheffield now for her firm —she must have volunteered to come—so she visits the site often, and as I told you she's there this week-end.'

' She may be just chasing him.'

' Oh, Mother—*please*! Why won't you ever face the truth?'

Helen's eyes widened. She stood up slowly, the colour

139

drained from her face. Melanie was appalled at herself and immediately contrite.

'Mother, I'm sorry. I didn't mean it.' It had been wrung from her, she realized that. Her mother had offered a straw at which Melanie simply dared not clutch, much as she longed to.

Helen stood quite still for a moment. Melanie feared and expected tears when she saw the pained expression on her mother's face and the faint trembling of her lips.

'Please, Mother. I'm sorry, I didn't mean it. Have another cup of tea,' she urged.

Helen shook her head but sat down again. 'But you *said* it, didn't you? So it must have been in your mind. That's what you think of me, what you've always thought, that I can't face up to things. But it's not true. I can when I have to. You don't understand. We all have different natures, our individual way of reacting to things that happen, and who is to say which is the right way and which the wrong? Some people accept and resign themselves to fate readily. I don't. I don't give in until it really is inevitable. And I react emotionally, too, I know. But I'm not always wrong, Melanie.'

'I'm sure you're not, Mother. It was wrong of me to say what I did or to think it. It's just that, as you said, Father has always tried to protect you from the hard knocks, and has taught me to do the same, right from when I was a child.'

Helen frowned. 'I didn't realise to what extent.'

Melanie tried to make light of it. 'Anyway, I'm so glad we've had this talk, Mother. With regard to Drew, I'm quite sure it's hopeless. He likes me well enough— at least I think he does. Which makes it even worse. I sometimes think it might be a better sign if he disliked me. I'm sure Stephanie wouldn't keep coming if he discouraged her, and why should she lie about Drew and herself? No, Mother, the only thing I can do is get right away. I suppose I shall get him out of my system one day—though I doubt it.'

Helen rose and picked up the breakfast tray. 'My dear, the only way you'll get a man like Drew out of your system is to fall in love with someone else, and I don't suppose you'll do that in a hurry. Anyway, you and he are made for each other, I'm sure of it.'

' Now, Mother—'

' You leave me to my optimism. You can be pessimistic if you like, though I think it's a mistake.'

Melanie sighed and shook her head. 'Mother, you won't say anything to anyone?'

' About you and Drew, you mean? Good heavens, of course not.' Then with a slow smile: ' I shan't have to. You'll see. Er—I take it it's all right to mention your other plans?'

Melanie nodded. ' Father will have to know some time.'

Her mother went out and Melanie looked after her with a fond expression, grateful for the better understanding between them. Then she sighed. If only she could share her mother's optimism about Drew! But it was no use building up any false hopes. He admired her for what he called her talents—modest enough in her own estimation, but he probably neither liked nor disliked her.

Her mind switched to Stephanie and Eric. Eric had admired Stephanie the first time he ever saw her. But there were men like that, who could admire a woman superficially and want to kiss and embrace them without having any depth of feeling for them. He had behaved that way towards herself. Or had tried to. There were women like that too, of course. Perhaps Stephanie was one of them, and there had been nothing in what she had seen beyond a mild flirtation. She hoped so for Drew's sake. All the same, if Stephanie were that kind of girl—

She threw back the bedclothes and tried to put the matter out of her mind. When she had bathed and dressed she tidied out her drawers and wardrobe, throwing away or putting aside for the next church jumble sale all those items past their best. Before long her mother called out that she was going shopping, and as soon as she had finished her task Melanie went downstairs and played the piano, first practising scales and arpeggios, then the section of the Grieg she had been working on previously. She found her fingers a little stiff, and knew with something like despair in her heart that she really had a long way to go before she could become a professional pianist. It was going to be expensive. Hours of daily practice were going to be essential. Could she do it? She would have to buy a piano for her flat, she would have to earn enough money on which to live— part-time in the shop or something like that.

She struck a wrong note, and with a sudden feeling of panic and hopelessness she left the piano and crossed to the window with its familiar view of the valley and the church. Was she going to be able to do it, or would it turn out to be no more than a pipe-dream? Perhaps the most important question of all was *why* she wanted to do it. Out of her love of music, a passionate desire for professional status and fame? Or merely as a substitute for Drew's love?

She turned away from the window fiercely. Whatever the motive which drove her, she must have something. Life would never be the same now. She could not possibly go on as before, working in her father's shop, giving the occasional charity concert interspersed with a pleasant social life. Neither could she live next door to Drew married to another woman. It would be impossible. And if she had her own place she *must* have a piano. But it would have to be a good one. A cheap, second-hand one would not do, she would have to buy a new one. It would take all her savings, but she would simply have to have one. Perhaps she could take in pupils, teach to help pay for her own studies.

Feverishly, almost, she made plans. She would continue to do some performances for charity, but she would let it become known that she was available for professional work. She *must* perfect the Grieg. She must. It was perhaps the most popular concerto of all.

She went to the piano again, and with fierce determination crashed out the inspiring opening chords. She must find a flat and get a piano *now*, as soon as possible, her thoughts still raced on. She was wasting time staying at that hotel, she was not getting any practice. She would have to see the building through, naturally, and she felt bound to help Drew with his, but she could drive to and from the site from her flat and get in some practice in the evenings.

After lunch she searched the local newspaper for advertisements for flats, but when she rang to enquire about the ones she saw she considered they were too expensive, besides which they were furnished, and she would want one unfurnished. With a sigh she replaced the receiver. It was not going to be as easy as she had imagined. Some people might object to a piano being played at all hours, for instance. She would have to make quite sure that there would be none. Complete freedom to practise without the feeling that one might be disturbing someone was essential. Perhaps she could enlist the help of her mother in finding the right place.

Her mother was surprised that she wanted to find a flat so soon, but promised to do what she could.

'Your father and I will help you with the furniture, of course,' she said.

'And if you really feel you must go on with this,' her father added, 'I can buy you a piano.'

But Melanie would not hear of this. 'No, no, Father, thanks all the same. I want to make my own way, but a few odd items of small furniture you can spare from home I would be glad of. And I really must go on with it, Father. Already my fingers are not as supple as they were, from lack of practice.'

Back at the building site on Monday morning Drew asked what she did over the week-end.

'Played the piano mostly,' she told him.

'Yes—' he said thoughtfully, 'you must have missed your music out here. Er—don't feel obliged to carry on with this project, you know. Call it a day any time you want. Now that we've got going and become organised I could manage. Did you see Eric, by the way?' he asked casually.

'Er—yes,' she answered truthfully. 'I trust you and Stephanie had a nice time together.'

'Oh yes.'

Melanie glanced at him covertly. Was it her imagination or did he look a trifle strained? But a man would surely look more than strained if the woman he were engaged to broke it off.

The following weeks, however, showed clearly that Stephanie had not broken off their engagement. She visited Drew at the site frequently, sometimes bringing with her an old pair of jeans and making a great pretence of helping, though Melanie observed that she helped precious little. What *was* evident, however, was the great personal interest she showed in Drew's house, and which could only mean one thing. She was going to be its mistress. Eric came from time to time, and Melanie could not help noticing that his visits invariably put Drew in a bad humour.

One day Melanie tackled Eric about seeing him with Stephanie. His eyebrows shot up.

'Me? With Stephanie? Where—and when?' She told him and he shook his head. 'Not me, old dear. Must have been somebody else. I mean—couldn't have been either of us.'

'Why not?'

'Why not?' he echoed. 'Well, she's gone on Drew, isn't she?'

Melanie drew in her breath. 'Eric, I couldn't have

been mistaken about both of you, could I?'

He shrugged. 'Oh, I don't know. You could have been. I mean, you must have been. Anyway, why didn't you speak if you thought it was us?'

'You were in a very close embrace.'

'Ah, so you couldn't see our faces?'

'No, but—'

'There you are, then.'

Melanie did not argue any more. She was still quite certain that the pair had been Eric and Stephanie, but it was evident that neither wanted it known.

It was some weeks before Helen succeeded in finding a suitable flat for Melanie. But at last she and Richard came to visit the site with the news.

'I found it through someone in the music club,' Helen said excitedly. 'It's not exactly a flat, but I think it will suit your purpose better. It's part of a house *and* it's furnished with a lovely piano in one room—a baby grand.'

'Really? Sounds too good to be true,' laughed Melanie.

'Well, my dear, with all the musical people we know, it was only a case of perseverence and patience. Actually, you'd be doing these people a favour. It's a fairly large house, too big for the owner—a Mr Fairfield—and his sister who keeps house for him. But he didn't want to sell it for sentimental reasons. It has such happy associations with his wife, you see. She was a pianist. Hardly anyone has played since his wife died three years ago, and he would love to hear it played again.'

'But suppose I wanted to give lessons?'

'Would you want to, dear?' queried Helen. 'Anyway, I shouldn't think there'd be any objection to that. His wife gave lessons, so he'll be well used to it. There's a lovely big bedroom upstairs you can have, and a sitting room downstairs next door to the old butler's pantry you can use as a kitchen. The piano is in a room by itself.'

'I—can hardly believe it,' Melanie said dazedly.

'Hardly believe what?' Drew said, joining them.

Before Melanie could say anything Helen was putting Drew completely in the picture. Melanie watched the surprise grow on his face. He looked at her, his brows knit together in a puzzled frown.

'But what is all this? I didn't know you had anything of this nature planned.'

Helen's hand flew to her mouth. 'Oh-h! You mean Melanie didn't tell you?'

'I'm sorry, Drew,' Melanie said swiftly. 'I—I meant to tell you, but—well, we've been so busy.'

'Yes, I supppose we have,' he said stiffly. His glance flicked over Richard and Helen. 'Before you go there are one or two things I'd like to discuss with you, if you don't mind.'

He strode back to the house that was to be their home. Helen looked after him worriedly.

'I do hope he isn't offended. I'm sorry, darling, but it didn't occur to me you hadn't told him.'

Melanie sighed. 'It's all right, Mother. I've been going to, but I—I suppose I kept funking it.'

Richard rose. 'I don't know what all the fuss is about. I'll go and see what it is Drew wants to discuss and leave you two to your machinations.'

'Your father doesn't know how you feel about Drew, of course,' Helen said as she watched her husband walk away. 'So he can't possibly understand.'

'I'm a fool,' muttered Melanie miserably.

'My dear, women in love often are.'

'I'm a coward, too. I should have told Drew what my plans were. He'd be interested—and of course he can't know how I feel about him. He asked me the first time he heard me play whether I'd ever thought of taking up music professionally. But of course he'll think the same as you did at first—that I could practise at

146

home. That's why I've put off telling him.'

'Of course,' murmured Helen sympathetically. 'I understand. Most difficult for you under the circumstances. But have a talk with him as soon as you can. He'll appreciate it, I'm certain.'

Melanie was not so sure, but she did feel she owed him an apology and some kind of explanation. When her parents had gone she went in search of him.

He was upstairs in what was to be the main bedroom, working swiftly with a roller, covering the walls with a priming coat of emulsion paint in a delicate shade of pink. He gave her the briefest of glances, then concentrated on what he was doing. Melanie felt wretched and was sorely tempted to go away again. But that would be sheer cowardice and she knew it.

'Drew, I'm sorry,' she jerked out.

'For what?' he asked without either pausing or taking his eyes from the broad swathes of pink appearing on the colourless plasterboard walls.

'For—not telling you about my plans,' she persevered.

'You're under no obligation to tell me anything you don't want to,' he answered coolly.

Melanie drew a deep breath, then she let out angrily: 'You're not making it very easy for me, are you?'

At this he swung around and dropped his roller into the tray of paint.

'I'm sorry,' he said abruptly.

He came slowly towards her and looked into her face searchingly, but Melanie turned and crossed to the window in case he should see the tears of frustration gathering in her eyes.

He stood where she had left him. 'Was there anything else in addition to what your mother has already told me—that you're going to study to take up music professionally and have a place of your own in town?'

'No-o, not really.'

'Then why couldn't you have told me yourself? I'd

have been interested, you know that,' he said, his voice now less cold.

Melanie gazed unseeingly through the window. *Interested*. His interest, when she wanted with all her heart his love.

'What I can't understand,' he went on, 'is why you can't pursue your music from here—from your own home. Why do you want a flat in town?'

She swung round, her control snapping. 'Because I do, that's why. I—I don't have to account to you for what I do!'

She walked swiftly to the door, but he barred her way. He gripped her by the shoulders and looked straight into her eyes now brimming with tears.

'Melanie—' he said in a voice so gentle it hurt. 'Melanie, you're not happy. Is it—to do with Eric?'

For a split second she stared at him. In another moment she would blurt out the truth.

'Yes—' she shot out in a panic. 'It *has* to do with Eric. He's in love with someone else, and to be given friendship when you want a man's love is—is something you'll never know or understand. I'm going to work as I've never worked before. I'm going to travel if I get the chance. So now you know it all, and I hope you're satisfied!'

She pushed past him and ran down the stairs. She knew she was behaving stupidly, but she didn't care. She jumped into her car, and as the engine revved, she fancied she heard Drew calling after her, but she paid no heed. All she wanted to do now was get away, to put as much distance as possible between herself and him. She did not drive to the hotel, but made for home. She would go to see Mr Fairfield first thing in the morning and if everything was all right, move in as soon as possible.

Naturally enough her parents were very surprised to see her. They had not long arrived home themselves.

'There's nothing wrong, is there?' her mother enquired anxiously.

Melanie shook her head. 'Not really.'

'And what is that supposed to mean?' Helen asked giving her a keen scrutiny. 'Did you have your talk with Drew?'

Richard put down his newspaper. 'I think I'll go and make a cup of coffee. I expect Melanie could do with one—and I daresay you could drink another.'

Melanie smiled wanly. 'I think he's being tactful. He once gave me a little talk about men and marriage—something like that, and said I should talk to you.'

Helen frowned a little. 'Why? Were you having trouble? Surely you could have talked to me.'

Melanie shook her head. 'We were just talking generally, that's all.'

'I see. Well, what happened to make you come home so unexpectedly?'

Melanie shook her head again involuntarily. She did not want to talk about it. But as briefly as she could she explained.

'I—I did try to talk to him as you suggested. I felt I owed him some sort of an apology, anyhow. But he didn't accept it very well.'

'Was he offended that you hadn't mentioned any of your plans?'

'I—suppose so. At any rate he was very cool. But it wasn't that which—upset me. It was the way he—didn't seem to care. Anyway, he asked the very question I expected him to—why couldn't I practise my music from home? I just didn't know how to answer him. In another minute I would have told him the truth.'

'Why didn't you?' her mother asked quietly.

Melanie looked at her in astonishment. 'What—tell him I was in love with him? Mother! I've got *some* pride left. As it is, I'm more emotional and—and irrational than I've been at any time in my life. I couldn't possibly have told him the truth of why I must get away and couldn't possibly live next door to him. Anyway, what good would it have done? As it was I was in danger of weeping on his shoulder, so I—just got in my car and drove home.'

'Without telling him?'

'Yes. My one thought was to escape, to get away from him, to see this flat or whatever it is you've found for me and—and start on my new life, as it were as soon as possible. I—thought I could go along and see Mr Fairfield in the morning.'

'Yes, dear, of course,' Helen said on a sigh. She was about to say something else when the telephone rang. 'I'll answer it,' she said, and went into the hall.

Melanie rose and stood looking out of the window, thinking how her whole life had changed since that morning she had first seen Drew. Would she ever know happiness or peace of mind again? Only through her music, she was sure.

In a few minutes her mother was back. 'Melanie, dear, it's Drew.'

CHAPTER VIII

' Oh, no!'

Her mother eyed her steadily. ' Shall I tell him you don't want to speak to him?'

Melanie gave a helpless gesture. ' I don't want to, but—but I suppose I'd better.'

' Yes, I should, dear. Actually, he was very worried about you. He'd rung your hotel—there was something he wanted to speak to you about—and when they said you hadn't come in—'

Melanie braced herself and went to speak to him. In love or not, she really would have to stop behaving so irrationally.

' Are you all right, Melanie?' was his first question.

' Yes, of course. I'm sorry I dashed off without telling you, but—'

' That's all right. I just wanted to say that if you would prefer not to go on with the building programme, it will be quite all right with me. In fact, it might be better if you did take a little time off. You certainly haven't been looking too well lately.'

' Drew, will you stop being so concerned about me!' she told him raggedly, then immediately regretted it. But she couldn't keep on apologising. There was a long silence, and at last Melanie felt she had to say something. ' I'm sorry, Drew,' she said in spite of herself. ' I just got into the car and drove off without thinking.'

' There's no need to apologise, Melanie,' he said firmly. ' I quite understand.'

Do you? Oh, Drew, if only you did, spoke her agonised mind.

' What I wanted to say,' he went on, in an odd sort of distant, remote voice, ' is that if you want to start working towards your musical profession right away, you probably would prefer not to spend any more time at the building site. You've been a tremendous help—I don't really have to tell you that—but your parents' house is well on the way to being completed now, and as I have the telephone—'

'But—but, Drew, what about *your* house? I really do feel I ought to help with that after all you've done on ours. I hadn't intended—'

'I've told you before, Melanie,' he cut in sharply, 'don't feel *obliged*. I don't want you to feel under any obligation whatever. If you're aiming to become a professional pianist you don't want to stiffen up your fingers by holding a paintbrush and things of that sort. You need full-time practice. You, of all people, should know that.'

'But I was going to do it gradually, not all at once and straight away, and I *want* to help with your house.'

'No,' he said brusquely, 'I won't have it. There's no hurry with regard to mine, so I shan't expect to see you here again except as a visitor.'

To Melanie it was clear that he no longer wanted her help. He was giving her no choice. She felt rather as she had on another occasion—that he had slammed a door in her face.

'All right, Drew,' she said bleakly. 'It shall be as you say. Goodbye.'

'Goodbye, Melanie—and good luck.'

That sounded more final than ever. Feeling utterly dejected, she rang off. For a few moments nothing seemed worthwhile, not even her music. The future without Drew was a vast, dark void. Then her mother called out to her, and she squared her shoulders and went back into the living room.

Naturally, her mother wanted to know the gist of her conversation with Drew, and Melanie made as light of it as possible. Helen took a cue, as it were, from her.

'Well, I think he's perfectly right. If you've made

up your mind to become a professional pianist you've no more time to waste in house-building. If you need any money you can always come to either me or your father. Or, if you would prefer it, help out in the shop one or two days.'

And so it was left at that. Melanie realised that determination was the only thing that was going to help her now, and she spent the rest of the day practising, which henceforth she would call 'working'.

The next morning she went to see Mr Fairfield and found everything was exactly as her mother had said. There was a room which held little else except a baby grand piano, a medium-sized room which she was assured was seldom if ever used, and which she could have as a living room, doing her cooking and washing up in the butler's pantry. Upstairs was a large bedroom overlooking the garden. She considered herself very lucky indeed to have been found such a place, and the rent Mr Fairfield was asking was ridiculously low.

He was a small man with silvery grey hair, a small moustache and a kind, gentle manner.

'But, Mr Fairfield,' Melanie said, ' are you sure you're asking enough rent for—for so much?'

'Yes, my dear, quite sure. Why should I ask more? You'll be doing me a favour—and my sister. A piano needs to be played or it becomes a thing without a soul. As for the other rooms, you'll be keeping them aired.'

'But shan't I disturb you by my constant playing? And would you mind if I took in pupils? That, at least, wouldn't be very nice for you.'

Mr Fairfield shook his head. 'You don't know how happy both of those things will make me. It's what I've missed these past years. The house will come alive again. In fact, I really shouldn't be taking anything from you at all, but I know how independent you modern girls like to be.'

Melanie could scarcely believe it. His sister, Miss

Emily Fairfield, a few years younger than her brother but very like him, echoed everything he said.

'My dear, it will be very nice to have you about the house. And when you're famous, we shall feel we've played some small part in your success.'

Melanie moved into her new home that same week. When she went to the hotel to collect her luggage and pay her bill she was sorely tempted to call at the site to see Drew, but decided against it. The less she saw of him the sooner she would get him out of her system. And that she *must* do.

There was ample room in the spacious wardrobe and drawers for all her clothes, and some bookshelves, kindly emptied by Emily Fairfield for Melanie, held all her books and some of her music. The piano was in beautiful tone. The first evening of her arrival Melanie played some favourite pieces for the benefit of the Fairfields, then the next day she began serious study of her scales, arpeggios and the Grieg concerto. She put an advertisement in the *Derbyshire Times* announcing that she was now able to take a limited number of pupils and that she was free to accept professional engagements. She was not yet ready to perform the concerto in public, but she had a fairly large repertoire of other compositions she had perfected and polished for public performance.

For some weeks it seemed that no one wanted either lessons or performances. Perhaps summer was a bad time. Certainly people, in general, preferred to spend more time out of doors, and in the summer months there were fewer concerts. To pay her rent, buy food, and pay for her own studies with her music master under whom she was working on the concerto, Melanie continued to draw on money she had saved. But it was getting dangerously low, when at last one morning she received an urgent telephone call from an agent who wanted someone to take the place the very next day of a pianist who was due to play at Cutler's Hall but who had suddenly been taken ill.

'What was she going to play?' asked Melanie.

'Schumann,' he answered promptly. 'And all works I've heard you do at charity concerts.'

'You've heard me play?'

'Certainly. It's my business to keep in touch with the musical scene. I was not surprised to learn you were turning professional. You should have done it years ago. Why don't you let me handle your engagements?'

Melanie laughed a little shakily. 'There haven't been any to handle yet.'

'There will be,' he promised. 'What are you working on now? Anything in particular?' She told him. 'A very good choice,' he said. 'It's popular. As soon as you're ready just let me know. It would be best if your first performance of it was at a charity concert and I'd arrange good press coverage for you.'

'That all sounds very businesslike.'

'You have to be. That's why it's better for artistic people like you to have an agent.'

'All right,' agreed Melanie, 'but I warn you, I haven't much money.'

'You pay me nothing until *you* have been paid, and you sign a contract before every performance.'

'Sounds fine.' It sounded almost too good to be true.

'You can do this job tomorrow, then?' he queried.

'Why—yes, of course.'

'Good. I'll have a contract drawn up and bring it round to you to sign in about an hour's time.'

Melanie put the telephone back on its cradle and hurried to tell Mr Fairfield and his sister the incredible news.

'Splendid, my dear,' the old man beamed. 'But what's so incredible about it? You really are good. Don't you realise that?'

'You really think so?'

155

Excitedly, she went off again to ring home and tell her parents, who naturally were absolutely delighted.

' We *must* find out if there are any tickets left—there probably will be—and of course your father will drive you there. You can't possibly drive yourself,' Helen said.

When she had rung off Melanie hesitated. Should she ring Drew? He would be pleased to know, she felt sure. She lifted the receiver then put it back again slowly. No, she mustn't. Wounds did not heal by constantly reopening them. She must have as little contact with him as possible.

At the thought of Drew her happiness was clouded for a little while, but as she forced herself to think of the forthcoming concert she sat down at the piano and began to play some of the Schumann pieces she had played at charity events and which might be those advertised for tomorrow's concert. She became so absorbed that in no time at all, it seemed, the agent, John Kenyon, arrived with the contract.

' There you are, Miss Lawrence—and I can't tell you how relieved and delighted they are in Sheffield to have got such a good replacement. I told them they were lucky to get you.'

Melanie smiled at this typical agent's exaggeration, but she liked the man and was glad of the opportunity to meet him. She was also more than pleased with the performing fee she was to receive as well as with the programme, a copy of which he had brought for her. The Schumann pieces she was to play were all ones which she knew well.

' By the way,' he said before he left, ' I saw you were advertising for pupils, too. Have you got many yet?'

' None at all,' she said ruefully.

' Well, speaking as your agent, that's probably a good thing. I don't know what you had in mind, but I certainly wouldn't advise you to take on raw beginners.

In fact, you might not have time for teaching at all after tomorrow's event. But if you should take on any pupils, have a limited number only and those whose playing is already to a good standard but who want to improve on their technique.'

Melanie promised, beginning to get a real thrill out of being treated like a professional.

When he had gone she went over the Schumann pieces again to satisfy herself about her general technique, then washed her hair and had an early night.

Cutler's Hall was not quite full, but reasonably so for a summer concert. Other artists in the programme were a solo cellist, a string quartet and a tenor singer. Melanie wished she had been first on the programme in one sense as she was a little nervous. So much depended on her giving a good, if not an outstanding performance on this, her first professional engagement. But the solo pianist had been billed last, and the order had not been changed. She followed the tenor who received a sufficient volume of applause to warrant an encore. When he had taken his final bow the producer explained to the audience that she had agreed at very short notice to take the place of the pianist billed who was ill, then Melanie walked on.

She had decided to wear white, a long dress with a full flowing skirt, and her hair on this occasion she had left long and straight. She acknowledged the polite ripple of preliminary applause, then went to the piano. Without thinking she tucked her hair behind her ears and as she touched the keys all her nervousness vanished in her love of the music. The piano had a beautiful tone and responded in a way which thrilled and delighted her.

She played three pieces and received a moderately sustained volume of applause. The producer of the concert, however, signalled ' no encore ' to her and the first half of the concert was over.

She remained in the artists' room during the interval and after a little while was joined by her parents, who told her she had made a very good performance.

'People are talking about you, darling,' murmured Helen. 'They're saying you were good, and an excellent substitute. I wouldn't be surprised if you got an encore in the second half.'

Melanie laughed. 'You're a sweetie, Mother—but I don't think so.'

'We're very, very proud of you, anyway,' her father said, giving her a kiss.

'Mother—' Melanie murmured just before they went back to their seats, 'I—wonder if Drew knows?'

Helen gave her a swift glance. 'You really should have rung and told him, darling.'

'I wanted to, but—'

'Never mind. Perhaps next time. Off you go now—and good luck for the second half.'

'Thanks.'

Now, Melanie was regretting that she had not rung Drew. He would have been pleased to know, and she suddenly realised that in spite of the existence of Stephanie, she would have given anything for Drew to have shared this important event of her life—her foot on the first rung of her professional career.

She heard the tenor begin his first song, and went and waited in the wings. He was allowed an encore for the second time that evening, but Melanie felt there was barely enough sustained applause to warrant it. Obviously this man was well known to Cutler's Hall concert-goers, even a favourite, perhaps.

Taking a deep breath, she walked on to the platform to begin her own final selection. The applause which greeted her was gratifyingly more than the previous time, and Melanie sat down at the piano considerably pleased. The first of her two pieces was the simple but effective *Traumerei*, the second, the delicate, haunting, and rather intricate *The Prophet Bird*.

The applause which followed came as a thrilling surprise. Melanie bowed a couple of times, then left the platform. As the applause continued, the producer nodded to her to take another bow. Again she left the platform, but the applause continued and to her astonishment one or two calls of 'encore—encore'. Melanie looked at the producer.

'Can you do another Schumann?' he enquired.

She nodded and walked back on to the platform to the piano, smiling to herself. Why not be unconventional and play an extract from the first movement of the concerto in A minor? It was one of her favourite arrangements.

She struck the first *forte* chord, and with a thrill of excitement continued with the exciting opening. The music had the same haunting, romantic quality of all Schumann's work and the changes in harmony and metre which gave it an added interest. When the last chords came down the applause which followed was quite deafening and one or two enthusiasts rose from their seats. She had to return to the platform three times to acknowledge the applause. But the producer would permit no more encores. On the third acknowledgement he escorted her on to the platform himself and held up his hand.

'Ladies and gentlemen, I think you will agree that that extract from Schumann's concerto is a most fitting end to the evening's music, and I am sure you will have many more opportunities of hearing Miss Lawrence play.'

She was met in the artists' room by John Kenyon, absolutely beaming.

'My dear Miss Lawrence, congratulations. I must confess I'm not a great lover of Schumann myself, but playing that arrangement from the concerto was a stroke of genius—an inspiration. It gave the audience a taste of what you really can do. You won't lack engagements after this, I can assure you.'

Her parents embraced her warmly. 'Congratulations,

darling, I knew you'd be a success,' murmured Helen.

' You deserve it,' her father said. ' This is no overnight success. You've worked hard on your music for years. It's high time you had wider recognition. You've been well up to professional standard for a very long time.'

The other artists congratulated her, too, and a number of people from the audience. It was all very exciting, but Melanie would have given anything for Drew to have been there.

Reporters and photographers, sensing a story and a new star performer, crowded the room. John Kenyon allowed some photographs and a few questions, then ushered them firmly out.

' I can tell you the rest, gentlemen. Miss Lawrence needs to rest now.'

Melanie said laughing, when he returned: ' I thought the idea was to get as much publicity as possible?'

He smiled knowingly. ' They've got all they want for the present, you'll see. It's my job to protect you from the pressure of these newshounds. It doesn't do to be too '' available ''. You have to give the impression of being—shall we say—precious, rather elusive, even mysterious.'

' And at the same time get lots of valuable publicity?' laughed Melanie. ' I'm afraid it's all too subtle for me.'

' It can be done,' John Kenyon said blandly. ' Just leave it to me and my P.R.O.'

He proved absolutely right on all counts. The newspapers the following morning all contained a photograph of Melanie accompanied by reports of the concert praising her performance with enthusiasm, telling of her years of devotion to music as an amateur and predicting a great future for her as a professional.

' Mind you,' he said to her over the telephone, ' just because you played Schumann at your debut you mustn't become known as a Schumann player. How's your Chopin? Most people like his works. I've heard you play some, but could you give a full Chopin recital?'

'Yes, I think so,' she answered, feeling rather bemused at the way everything seemed to be happening so suddenly.

'Good. We'll arrange a popular programme and you can do a series of them in all the main provincial towns. Then London when I've got enough press notices. Meanwhile, be ready as soon as you can with the Grieg.'

'I'm in your hands,' she said weakly.

Melanie thought he sounded over-confident. Nevertheless, she worked exclusively on the Grieg and as a relaxation played regularly a selection chosen from Chopin's waltzes, studies and nocturnes—some for their melody or for their popularity and others for their difficulty of technique.

A number of parents brought their young children to her to learn to play the piano shortly after the concert, also some young adults who wanted to study further, but the majority of these she felt compelled to turn away. She was beginning to realise she was not going to have much time to spare for giving lessons, also that teaching and being a concert pianist were two entirely different things. Events, once begun, had moved far more swiftly than she had ever imagined. Two sixteen-year-olds, however, pleaded so much, she promised to hear them play and try to set them on the right road, though she would not be able to give them regular lessons if she were to travel around the country giving recitals.

The next six months were the most hectic Melanie had ever known in her life. She gave Chopin recitals in Leeds, Hull, Manchester, York, and many more cities besides, both in Scotland and Wales. Finally she played in London, and in addition, appeared on television on a Saturday evening show. It was on this show that she played the first movement of the Grieg concerto—she had skipped the proposed charity performance of it. Three weeks later she was asked to play the whole concerto in London—again as a substitute for a soloist who had been taken ill.

'I seem to specialise in being a substitute,' Melanie said ruefully.

'Nonsense,' returned John Kenyon. 'It happens all the time. You know this pianist well, don't you?'

'Yes, I've heard her play the concerto often—and she does it beautifully. If I'm half as good—'

'You'll be as good, if not better. Actually, she's becoming exhausted. She's been doing too much. Her agent knew you were available. I told him a long time ago—just in case.'

'Very clever of you.'

Never far from her thoughts, Melanie thought with sudden yearning of Drew. This time she really must send him a ticket—that is, if he would come. Or ought she to send him two—one also for Stephanie? At this thought despair filled her heart once more.

'What's the matter?' asked John Kenyon. 'You look sad all at once.'

She tried to smile. 'Nothing. But could you get me some tickets for the concert?'

'Of course. Two for your parents?'

'Four altogether. There are—two other people who might like to come. Friends of mine.'

But she hoped fervently that Stephanie would not come. She even half hoped Drew would not, yet wanted him to, and longed to see him.

By this time her parents had moved into their new house. Melanie had been over there, but Drew had been away. His house was completed, too. At least the actual building was, but Drew had been away. Decorators were busy inside, and through the windows Melanie caught a glimpse of panelled walls, but she did not go inside.

On the evening of the concert Melanie booked a room for her parents at the same hotel where she herself was staying. John Kenyon, who now called himself her manager, was also staying there.

'Are you feeling nervous at all, Melanie?' her father asked as they all ate a light meal together before going to the concert hall.

'Well, just a little,' she admitted. 'Have you heard from Drew, Mother? Do you know whether he's coming?'

'He wasn't sure whether he could make it,' answered her mother. 'He's doing a job up North at the moment.'

'I see.'

John enquired who Drew was and gave Melanie a keen look. 'You know, after this concert I think you should take a rest. Christmas is only three weeks away, and I'm arranging a tour of Europe for you in the early part of the year, as you know. I don't want you getting overtired. Besides, you'll need a few weeks' preparation. And furthermore, young lady, I suggest you stay at home with your parents. You need someone to look after you. You're a very valuable commodity now, you know.'

'Thanks, I'm sure,' Melanie told him, forcing a laugh.

Later, her mother whispered to her, 'John is right, my dear. You do need a rest at home. And you needn't worry about Drew. His house isn't ready for occupation yet, and not likely to be until he's finished on the job up North.'

The Grieg was the second item in the programme. In the artists' room Melanie listened to the opening bars of the Merry Wives of Windsor overture, then began to gather herself together. She was about to go along the corridor leading to the platform to stand ready, when an official brought her a note. The handwriting was vaguely familiar. She tore it open and breath seemed to leave her body as she saw the signature. It was from Drew. It said: *I won't wish you luck, Melanie. You won't need it. You're going to give the performance of your life and be a great success. All that is left for me to wish you is joy and happiness in the future.* It was signed simply, *Drew.*

For a moment the joy and happiness he had wished upon her overwhelmed her. He had come! He was here. He had wanted to share in what would probably be the greatest moment of her career—her first professional performance of the whole of the Grieg piano concerto on a London concert platform. Her heart near to bursting, she walked along the narrow corridor and the next moment found herself being led on to the platform to face a veritable sea of faces. Somewhere out there, she thought, was Drew. Drew. She would play for him.

She needed no music. She knew every note off by heart. Her music master had given her the cues for coming in by playing his violin. At home she had a tape recording of the orchestration, and she had attended the rehearsals under this conductor and with the orchestra. She loved every note and every phrase and played as she had never played before.

When she had finished there was a moment of silence, then like a thunderclap the applause broke and rose to a volume Melanie knew spelled out success. As she bowed in acknowledgement an official brought on a sheaf of flowers. This was followed by another and then a basket. She caught sight of her parents and blew them a kiss, the entire orchestra rose to applaud, and three times she had to return to the platform to take a bow, and finally had to play some of the last movement again before the rest of the concert could continue.

She returned to the artists' room breathless and excited to find more flowers waiting for her. Some were from her mother and father, others from old friends, and best of all a dozen red roses from Drew. She breathed in their fragrance deeply. If only they would last for ever! People crowded into the room even though the rest of the concert was not over, but there was no sign of Drew.

'Did you see him, Mother?' she murmured as soon as there was an opportunity.

Helen shook her head. 'No, dear, I didn't. But perhaps he's waiting until the concert is over. It wouldn't do if everyone left their seats, would it?'

There was a bevy of reporters all asking questions. What were her plans for the future? What did it feel like to be a success overnight? And even: Had she any romance in her life, was she engaged or about to be?

John Kenyon came to her rescue. 'In the New Year, Miss Lawrence will be touring Europe. There is no such thing as success overnight. Miss Lawrence has only recently decided to become a professional.'

He ignored the question about romance in her life, but a woman reporter persisted:

'Are you engaged, Miss Lawrence?'

'No, I'm not,' she answered.

'Are you perhaps—in love? My readers—'

'That is entirely my own affair.'

'Would you give up your career for marriage?'

'The question doesn't arise.'

Melanie cast an appealing glance at John, who immediately ushered them away.

Only Helen knew what these questions meant to Melanie. 'Don't let them upset you, darling. Once you're in the public eye people are interested in you. They'll be wondering next if there's a romance between you and John.'

Melanie forced a smile. John was twenty years her senior, and though he was very good-looking and unmarried their relationship was entirely unromantic. Neither ever asked personal questions about the other.

When the concert was over more people came into the

room, a good many to congratulate Melanie, and at last when she had given up hope Drew appeared in the doorway. At the sight of him, so dear to her, her heart seemed to stop beating. She stood mute and it was like an age before he saw her and crossed the room.

He held out his hand to her and said gravely: ' Congratulations, Melanie. I knew you would do it.'

Slowly, she put her hand in his and looked into his face. Was it possible he did not know she loved him?

' Thank you,' she answered in a voice which sounded unnatural even to her own ears. ' I'm so glad you could come.'

' I wouldn't have missed it,' he said, and turned to speak to Helen and Richard. ' You're staying overnight in London?' he queried.

It was Richard who answered him. ' And you?'

' No, I'm catching a late train.' He glanced at his watch. ' If you don't mind, I'll be off. I only dropped in to have a word with Melanie.' He put a hand lightly on her shoulder. ' Keep in touch. I'll always be interested in what you're doing.'

Melanie stared after him feeling as if she had turned to stone. She meant nothing to him. Nothing at all. She was just someone he happened to know, someone in whose career he was interested, that was all.

She felt her mother's hand on her arm. ' Come along, dear, let's get back to the hotel. You look worn out. It was nice of Drew to come. Pity he couldn't have stayed a little while longer.'

John arranged for her flowers to be sent to the hotel, then they left the concert hall. Later, alone in her room, having retired for the night, Melanie could allow her thoughts to dwell on Drew for a little while as well as look back on her success. She recalled the question of the eager woman reporter, and her success paled beside her love for Drew. She buried her face in his roses. Thrilled and happy though she was about her success, she would give it all up gladly to marry Drew.

The national press the following day was full of praise for Melanie's performance. The telephone in her room at the hotel scarcely stopped ringing. Requests for interviews from magazine editors, for engagements to play at concerts, on television and even to advertise a particular brand of soap all poured in.

'It's worse than being a film star,' laughed Helen. 'I'd no idea that successful concert pianists were so sought-after.'

'It's partly because she's young—and beautiful,' John said surprisingly. He had never paid her a compliment of that nature before. But perhaps it was not as personal as it sounded. She had again worn white at the concert and her hair long as she had that first night in Sheffield, factors which undoubtedly made her look younger than she really was.

They caught a late afternoon train back to Chesterfield, then did the remainder of the journey by car. Melanie was glad to be home. She had not realised how badly she needed a rest.

'My dear, it's all the excitement as well as the travelling—not to mention the hard work you've put in on the piano,' her mother told her.

For a few days Melanie went to bed early and got up late and played the piano only at short intervals. It was odd now that when she sat down to play she felt she were at work. Her mother said the feeling would pass, but Melanie wondered. She also felt restless. Every time she looked through the window at the view—the gardens partly laid out, the river flowing below and the rise of the moors beyond she thought of Drew, and each time she thought of him it was with pain in her heart.

Then she was caught up in the pre-Christmas rush of shopping and other preparations, dinner parties at home and dinner parties with friends. At Christmas she had a card from Drew postmarked Windermere. So he was at home. And Stephanie? Melanie presumed she was back there, too. Of Eric she saw nothing at all, neither did she hear from him.

As soon as the Christmas season was over Melanie began work, this time on her repertoire in preparation for her Continental tour. As Drew was not in residence next door but still working up North, Melanie gave up her rooms with the Fairfields and stayed at home. She would have to think about the future later when her tour was finished.

Just three weeks after Christmas she set out for Paris where she was to give her first performance. As she had promised she sent a note to Drew telling him of the tour, at the same time telling herself that she was a fool. He was interested to a point, but she doubted whether he had *really* wanted her to keep in touch.

In Paris she played Chopin, in Germany Schumann. In several countries she played the Grieg, including Czechoslovakia, Spain and Italy. John Kenyon accompanied her, and it was not very long before gossip columnists began to link their names together and hint of a romance between them.

' Idiots,' John said, as he read one particular column. ' Do you mind, Melanie?'

She laughed shortly and shook her head. ' No. It doesn't matter.'

He gave her a long look. ' Doesn't it? Are you sure? Isn't there some man back home who might be jealous?'

' I wish there were,' she answered off guard.

' The rather distinguished-looking fellow who gave you the red roses the first time you played the Grieg?'

She gave him a surprised look. ' You're very observant.'

He nodded. ' It's part of my job. I've a long memory, too. But what happened? Did you quarrel?'

' No. There never was anything beyond a certain

168

kind of friendship.'

John gave her a puzzled look. ' I find that hard to believe.'

' Why?' asked Melanie.

He gave a faint smile. ' Shall I tell you something? I'm half in love with you myself. Who wouldn't be? There isn't a single thing wrong with you. You have everything—a natural charm and grace, a lovely nature, talent—'

Talent. Melanie almost hated the word. ' You're being very sweet and complimentary, John, but that description could fit thousands of women. Besides, Drew was already engaged before I met him.'

' How long ago was that?'

' Last spring.'

' And he still isn't married?'

' Not so far as I know.'

' Well, what's the hold-up?'

' John, how should I know? I *do* know that he's built a house for her. It's next door to that of my parents. But please—can't we talk about something else?'

' Of course,' he said swiftly. ' I hadn't meant to pry. It's just that one thing leads to another once you get talking, doesn't it?'

' Yes, it does.'

They were in Naples and it was spring. Melanie looked at John across the table where they were having lunch at a hotel overlooking the glorious bay. He was a good man, a pleasant companion, and she appreciated his accompanying her on this tour. The rest of his clients he had left to his assistant, saying he would enjoy a trip on the Continent as much as he hoped she would.

' John—' she said suddenly, ' how is it that you yourself have never married?'

He shrugged and looked down at his plate. ' I've never met anyone I've liked well enough—or who has liked me sufficiently well.'

' Now that *I* find hard to believe,' she retaliated.

He looked up quickly, his brows arched. ' Really? Tell me more.'

She smiled, feeling suddenly lighthearted, even gay. ' Let me see now. You're an excellent companion, you're dependable, reliable. In fact you have all the qualities, in a masculine way, that you attributed to me.'

He was silent for a moment, then he said quietly: ' I wouldn't want a marriage based solely on qualities of mere companionship and reliability. I'd want—well, to be in love and the woman to be in love with me. Or do you think I'm too old for romance?'

On a sudden impulse she put out a hand to him across the table.

' John, what a silly thing to say! Of course you're not too old for romance. Why, I—'

John leaned towards her eagerly, but Melanie's attention was suddenly riveted to someone who had just entered the dining room.

It was Drew.

CHAPTER IX

At the precise moment that Melanie withdrew her hand swiftly from John's, Drew looked across the room and saw them.

'What's the matter?' asked John, seeing the startled expression on her face.

'It's—Drew.'

'Where?'

John turned his head sharply. Drew was just standing there, not moving, as if he were no more than part of a dream. Hesitantly, Melanie raised her hand and gave him a slight wave, but there was no response from him and her spirits sank.

'I—don't think he can see us,' she said.

John rose. 'Perhaps he doesn't want to intrude or something silly like that. I'll go get him.'

Or was he looking for someone else—for Stephanie? was Melanie's sudden, agonised thought. They might even be on their honeymoon.

Now John was talking to him, and from where Melanie was looking Drew appeared very reluctant to join them. He shook his head and half turned to walk away. Melanie's lips trembled. She was about to put her hand to them, but instead, to curb her emotions, she opened her handbag and took out her powder compact. Her hand shook so much she snapped the compact shut again and put it away. But the small action had helped in some degree, and all at once Drew was standing beside the table. Neither spoke for a moment, then Melanie put on a bright smile and spoke to him. She felt she simply dared not hold out her hand in case he should feel it trembling.

'Drew, this *is* a surprise!'

'Hello, Melanie,' he said rather gravely. 'You're

looking very well. Very well indeed, obviously enjoying life out here.'

'Oh yes. It's been a wonderful trip, so exciting and everything, and John—' John had signalled a waiter to bring another chair. 'You will join us, Drew, won't you?' she asked, ' unless—'

'Unless?'

'Well, I mean—are you alone, or—'

'I'm alone,' he said briefly.

He didn't look very happy, Melanie thought suddenly. Had something gone wrong with his engagement to Stephanie? Were she and Eric—

'Let me order some lunch for you,' John was saying. 'Melanie and I are only about half way through ours.'

'Yes, do,' urged Melanie, surprising herself by sounding more like someone being merely polite rather than someone whose heart was beating with warmth and love. 'And tell me all the news from home. Have you seen anything of Mother and Father recently?'

Drew nodded. 'I have, as a matter of fact. About a couple of weeks ago. I was—doing some jobs on the house.'

'Oh, really? I suppose it's all ready for occupation by now?'

'You could say that, I suppose,' he answered. 'All it needs is furniture, carpets and so on.'

'When do you expect to move in?' asked John.

Melanie waited on the brink of eternity for his answer, for some mention of Stephanie and his marriage.

But he said: 'My plans are rather uncertain as yet. I might follow Melanie's example and come over here to work. There are plenty of civil engineers required. Roads are still being built over mountains and across mountains. By the way, how is the tour going?' he went on before Melanie could make any comment on his news. 'And what plans have you for the future?'

'The tour has gone fine,' she told him. 'As to the

future—that's in John's hands.'

Drew looked startled. 'You really mean—'

John laughed and looked over his shoulder. 'Good thing there are no gossip columnists hanging around! They pick up the slightest whisper. News is news, but gossip can mean anything or nothing,' he said cryptically. 'Actually, Drew, we've just about finished this tour. We're here for about a couple of weeks—and that will include a holiday on Capri, then back home and another break. I'm making quite sure that Melanie doesn't flog herself to death. After that, she has several engagements lined up, mostly to play the Grieg. And then, I hope, an American tour.'

'And you'll be going with her?' queried Drew.

'Lord, yes. She's my star. Besides, you don't think I'd let her go alone, do you?'

Drew made no reply to this. He turned to Melanie. 'Will you be staying at home between tours or living in your flat?'

Melanie drew a long breath. 'At home for a little while, at any rate. But I won't be going back to the Fairfields' place.'

When Drew and Stephanie did move in next door to her parents, she would be able to afford a proper flat.

There was a short silence. There were many things Melanie longed to know but shrank from asking. One of these John asked for her.

'But what brings you to Naples at this time of the year?'

Drew looked swiftly from one to the other, then he answered abruptly: 'I like Naples.'

'And how long do you intend to stay?'

'I'm flying back tomorrow.'

'So soon?' asked Melanie without thinking. 'But when did you arrive?'

'A few days ago. But I have to get back.'

'Pressure of work?' queried John.

'No, just restlessness.'

Or Stephanie, thought Melanie with a swift pang. She wanted to ask him about Stephanie, why she hadn't come with him, when they were planning to get married. And yet she dreaded hearing the answers.

'A pity,' John went on. 'Actually, tonight is Melanie's final concert in Naples. We had planned to do a little sightseeing, then go over to Capri for a week or ten days.'

'Very nice.'

'I was wondering—' John mused, 'Melanie usually rests in the afternoons. It's pretty essential. But if you'd care to join us after the evening's concert—we usually have a light dinner and perhaps a little stroll—'

'Isn't it rather up to Melanie?' Drew answered brusquely.

'If—you've nothing else planned I'd love you to join us,' Melanie told him.

He gave her a fixed look, then shook his head swiftly. 'No, no, I think not, thanks.'

Melanie felt repulsed. There was a sudden constriction in her throat and her whole body tensed. She couldn't speak and she knew it would take all her will power not to burst into tears, strung up as she was.

'Won't you change your mind?' she heard John say. 'It would give Melanie an enormous amount of pleasure, I feel sure.'

At this she put her hand on Drew's arm. 'Yes, do— please, Drew.'

'In that case—thank you. It's very kind of you.'

In her suite at the hotel Melanie rested after lunch, then played the piano and had tea. Drew had said he would be at tonight's concert, then he and John would have dinner upstairs in Melanie's sitting room.

'Afterwards we can sit out on the balcony and watch the lights across the bay or maybe take a stroll,' said John.

Melanie had saved a rather special dress for her last appearance and hoped Drew would like it. It was not unlike the dress she had worn when he had taken her out to dinner that evening which seemed so long ago. It was white—which she always wore—with a swirling pattern in gold sequins and low cut to set off a sparkling necklace she had bought in Venice. She looked in the mirror and tried to see herself through Drew's eyes, but turned away abruptly as she thought of Stephanie.

Knowing this was her final appearance in Naples the audience gave her a tremendous acclamation. There were calls of *brava* and *ripetizione*, until in the end she decided to play the plaintive *Solveig's Song* in an effort to subdue them. Even so, as she took her final bow bouquet after bouquet of flowers were presented to her— and among them a dozen red roses which she knew instinctively were from Drew. These she took with her to the hotel, the rest John ordered to be sent later, and in the morning she would send most of them to the local hospitals as she always did—though she did not always receive quite so many as on this occasion.

John drove Drew and herself back to the hotel and there ushered them both into the lift, saying he would join them in a few minutes.

Alone with Drew Melanie felt nervous. In her suite he gazed all around with interest.

' You've come a long way, Melanie,' he said.

She smiled uncertainly. ' You think it's extravagant?'

' No—o. It's what you deserve. You've worked hard.'

' It was John's idea. And of course I *have* to have a piano.'

' Naturally. You don't have to explain.'

She invited him to sit down and asked him if he would like a drink before they ate.

' Have you got some up here?' he queried.

She nodded. ' John keeps some here—just in case

175

anyone calls.'

She felt his keen gaze follow her as she went to the cupboard where the drinks were kept, and almost wished John would come. She was finding it rather unnerving being alone with Drew.

He looked up at her when she returned with his drink and said unexpectedly:

'You're looking very, very beautiful—you know that?'

She drew a startled breath. 'Drew, really! You—you shouldn't say things like that.'

'Why not?'

'Well, I—'

There was a knock at the door. Melanie called out 'Come in,' expecting to see John. But a porter stood there with a note.

'For you, Miss Lawrence.'

It was from John saying he had met someone downstairs he felt he should talk to and asking her to excuse him. *'I'm sure you and Drew will have lots to talk about,'* he went on, *'so don't wait dinner for me, and I'll see you about eleven in the morning.'*

As the porter withdrew Melanie handed the note to Drew. He read it and handed it back to her.

'Does he often do this sort of thing?' he asked.

'What do you mean? What sort of thing? He often meets—'

'I meant leave you flat for the rest of the evening.'

'Of course not! I can absolutely rely on John. He always has a very good reason for what he does. And even if I'd been alone—which I'm not—what would it have mattered? I would simply have had an early night.' She glanced at her watch. 'If you can call ten-thirty an early night.'

'It is by Italian standards.' He finished his drink and set the glass down, then said speculatively: 'I must say you spring very readily to his defence.'

'Why shouldn't I?'

Drew stood up. 'Would you prefer that I leave you "to have an early night"?'

Suddenly she felt angry with him—angry for putting her in the position of having to ask him to stay, for being so blind, for Stephanie, angry out of sheer frustration and love for him.

'Dinner has been ordered for three. It will be here at any moment,' she answered, controlling her voice with difficulty.

To hide the pain and anger which must surely show on her face she went out on to the balcony. For a few moments she stood there alone, half expecting to hear the door open and close behind her. Then she became aware that he was standing behind her.

'Do you *want* me to stay, Melanie?' he asked in a low voice.

She rounded on him. 'Drew, of course I want you to stay! But, for goodness' sake, not unless you really want to.'

'I want to,' he answered softly.

Her anger subsided, but her heart began to do strange things. How wonderful he could be when he chose! His hand touched her shoulder and she almost passed into eternity. She half turned to him, and swiftly his lips touched hers. With an effort she prevented herself from flinging her arms about his neck and returning his kiss with all the passion which was rapidly welling up inside her. But the pressure of his lips increased and she pushed against him.

'Drew, please! There are certain people you seem to have forgotten,' she told him tremulously.

'Such as whom?'

'Stephanie—'

'Damn Stephanie,' he breathed in a caressing voice. 'Damn Stephanie, Eric, John, the lot of them. Just for tonight, let's forget them all.'

His arms came about her and she could no longer resist him. She lent herself to the sheer bliss of his lips on hers and his arms which wrapped around her. After a few minutes, however, there came a discreet knock on the door and she disengaged herself to call out 'come in'. A waiter entered with the dinner trolley. It was a meal for two. John must have changed the order.

The waiter set a table with a lace cloth, lit candles and served the soup. On the trolley was a bottle of champagne.

'With Mr Kenyon's compliments, *signorina*,' said the waiter.

'That should have been my pleasure. He thinks of everything, doesn't he?' came from Drew.

'You're our guest,' Melanie pointed out.

Drew smiled suddenly. 'So I am, so I am. Well then, I'll make the most of it.'

It seemed an odd remark to make, but Melanie put it out of her mind and told the waiter he could go.

'We'll help ourselves to the rest.'

He lifted silver covers and indicated lobster, cold chicken and salad, a delicious-looking sweet and a jug of cream. Coffee was gently percolating.

'You certainly do yourselves well,' remarked Drew. 'Is this what you call a light meal?'

'It's what the Italians call a light meal,' Melanie corrected. 'In any case, there's nothing heavy here.'

'True.'

It was all delicious and the champagne a perfect complement. Drew was gay and lighthearted, and Melanie did her best to forget Stephanie and tomorrow.

'What was the weather like at home when you left?' she asked him.

'Not bad, not bad at all. I think we may have a very nice early spring. You know—warm.'

'That will be something to look forward to. What about the—the gardens? Any progress there?'

She thought these " safe " kind of questions, but was not absolutely sure.

' Well—' Drew answered, ' your father has left a good deal of the meadow grass and is just having it mowed regularly. But then I suppose you know that.'

She smiled. ' I don't, actually. Mother writes the letters, and that's not the kind of thing she talks about. She talks about curtains and carpets, trips to town and having visitors.'

' Understandable. Anyway, he has flower gardens set out and lawn turf laid adjacent to the house.'

' And—yours?' she ventured foolishly.

He didn't answer for a moment. His face had clouded and he kept his gaze directed to his plate. Then he flashed a sudden, swift look at her and said roughly:

' Did you know that Stephanie and Eric are married?'

Her glass to her mouth, she all but choked. She stared at him wide-eyed.

' Oh, Drew—no!' she said in dismay. ' I—I didn't.' No wonder he didn't look too happy, and hadn't been when she had first seen him this morning, and no wonder he had wanted to forget Stephanie for a while. ' Drew, this is—terrible news. I—' She scarcely knew what to say. ' But I thought we were going to forget about them just for this evening?'

He gave her a long look, then smiled faintly. ' So I did. Sorry. You were asking me about my garden. For various reasons the work has slowed down, but at least I've had the terracing laid out as you had designed. But I'm rather losing—interest, so let's talk about something else.'

' Of course.'

She remembered now that he had talked of coming over to Europe to work. He must be feeling terribly unhappy. In an effort to help him she rose and crossed to a record player John had brought with them. She put on a selection of light music, and when a waltz was

179

played, she put out her hand to him and said: 'Let's dance.'

It was a strange but wonderful evening. They danced, in his arms and they danced to the dreamy sentimental tune.

It was a strange but wonderful evening. They danced, they finished the champagne, they sat out on the balcony and neither Eric nor Stephanie were mentioned again. At last Drew glanced at his watch and announced that he ought to go as it was long past midnight.

'Just play something for me before I go—if you're not too tired,' he pleaded.

She played a little Chopin, then Beethoven's haunting *Für Elise*. As she played the last note she felt Drew's hands caress her neck and follow gently the curve of her bare shoulders. She closed her eyes, savouring the joy of his touch. Then his hands gripped her fiercely and she felt his lips warm on the nape of her neck. She trembled.

'Drew—oh, Drew—'

She swung around and stood up and the next moment they were locked in each other's arms, all restraint gone. At any moment she expected to hear him say he loved her. No man surely could kiss like this if he were not in love and he must know now that she loved him. But with a great intake of breath he released her. For a moment he gazed at her, his eyes wide, then he said huskily:

'I'm sorry, Melanie. I—we both got carried away. I—I'd better go, otherwise—' He broke off abruptly. Then he gripped her shoulders hard and kissed her once more—fiercely, and muttering something like, 'See you in the morning' he went out swiftly.

For a moment she felt she couldn't move. She just stood there gazing at the door he had closed behind him, not knowing whether she was deliriously happy or in the depths of despair. Why had he kissed her like that, why?

But as she moved about the room and made preparations for bed, still feeling the touch of his lips the pressure of his arms, a sweet joy began to possess her. He was not the kind of man to kiss with such feeling and it not be genuine. And best of all, he was not going to marry Stephanie. Disquieting thoughts that he was still unhappy about his broken engagement, that he could have been kissing herself to give vent to his feelings about Stephanie, she thrust to the back of her mind. She drifted to sleep with a smile on her face and happiness in her heart.

She usually had breakfast in her room, but this morning when the maid brought in her tray there was a letter on it.

It was in Drew's hand. She tore it open excitedly, but when she read the contents she received a shock. It was brief and to the point. *Melanie: Am returning home by an early plane. Once more, my regrets for last night.*

My regrets for last night. The phrase repeated itself over and over again in her brain. He regretted it. Regretted it!

Leaving her breakfast untouched, she moved about the suite in an effort to control her emotions. She wished he had never come to Naples.

John came in at about eleven to have coffee with her as he always did. He looked at her tense face.

' What's the matter? Didn't you sleep?'

' Yes, I slept,' she answered dully. ' I slept very well indeed. What I did have is what is commonly called " a rude awakening". Read this.'

She passed Drew's note to him. John read it with a grimace.

' May one ask what happened last night?'

Melanie shrugged. ' Nothing really.'

' Then why—'

She sighed. ' Oh, John, what's the use? Whether or not you left us together purposely I don't know, but it

181

didn't work out.'

'Why not?' I was convinced that it would be best, that you ought to have some time alone together. I got to wondering why he had come to Naples just when you were here and—'

'And you came to the conclusion he had come because of me. Well, you were wrong.' She moved about the room restlessly. 'There was a little awkwardness between us at first, then we began to enjoy it. We danced, we sat out on the balcony, he kissed me—oh, it was all very romantic,' she told him bitterly.

John frowned. 'He didn't strike me as the sort of man who would make love to one woman while he was engaged to another.'

'Oh, he's not. He isn't engaged any longer. He told me. He kissed me not once but several times, and I—let my feelings show. That was when he started to apologise and—well, you've read his note. So that's that, John, and I don't want to talk about it any more. The sooner you can arrange that American tour the better I shall like it.'

John's eyebrows raised a fraction. 'That won't be any problem. After this European tour you'll be turning down more engagements than you can possibly accept. At this very moment there are several offers of American tours sitting right on my desk. But first, that holiday.'

Melanie said she didn't really feel much like a holiday. She would far rather be busy, but John insisted. He hired a car and drove her to a great many interesting places—Amalfi, Pompeii and Herculaneum, Vesuvius, Caserta and Benevento. It was all so interesting and John was such a wonderful guide and companion that for long periods she was able to dull her unhappy thoughts of Drew.

At the end of the third day of sightseeing, in fact, Melanie felt so tired when they returned to the hotel in

Naples, she said laughingly:

'I thought you said I needed a rest?'

'So you do. But first you needed—shall we say—a little mental recuperation. I think now we're ready to go over to Capri and there lie and soak up the sun and relax. Do you agree?'

She smiled at him fondly. How kind and gentle and understanding he was!

'Yes, I agree—and thanks.'

Capri was wonderful. John had booked a room for himself and a suite for Melanie overlooking the beautiful Marina Piccola and the rock of the Sirens. It was an enchanting island and John made it almost impossible for her to be anything but happy. They splashed about in the sea, sunbathed, explored the rest of the island, took a cable-lift up Mount Solaro from Anacapri and visited the famous Blue Grotto. Then in no time at all it was their last evening.

'Well?' queried John as they sat on Melanie's balcony in the soft warm evening after dinner. 'Have you enjoyed your holiday?'

'Oh, yes, John, I really have. It's been wonderful—thanks to you.'

'You look better for it, anyway,' he commented.

She gave him a warm smile. 'And you? You've enjoyed it, too, I hope.'

He put his hand on her arm. 'What a question! Of course I have. For two pins I'd ask you to marry me.'

For a split second she froze, then she relaxed and gave a mischievous smile. 'Why don't you?'

He shook his head. 'My dear, I wouldn't want to catch you on the rebound. But you're my kind of woman, Melanie, and that's the truth. If you're still without a husband in, say, a year's time, I'll be waiting.'

'Oh, but, John—' she began worriedly.

But he shook his head. 'Don't let it bother you. Just remember that I'll always be somewhere around.'

She could be happy with John, she knew that, but each time she thought of Drew a great yearning filled her heart.

The following morning they caught a jet plane from Naples and were home in time for dinner. John had driven her home from the airport, and her parents insisted on his staying the night.

Melanie was just about to slip between the sheets when her mother tapped on her door and opened it.

' Feel like a little chat—not too tired?'

Melanie smiled. ' Of course not, Mother. Come in—and I'll switch on the fire. It's not quite so warm here as it was in Capri.'

' I suppose not. Er—darling, do you mind if I ask you one or two questions?'

' Questions, Mother? What kind of questions?'

' Well, first, is there anything between you and John apart from a business association?'

' A romance, you mean?'

Helen regarded her steadily. ' Well? Is there?'

It was not an easy question to answer, knowing that John wanted to marry her.

She smiled at her mother teasingly. ' You know the stock answer to that, surely, Mother? We're just good friends.'

' Melanie, I'm not joking, and I don't want the stock answer. Let me ask you another. Are you still in love with Drew?'

Melanie closed her eyes and took a deep breath. ' Yes, Mother, I am, but it's no *use*! And I'm trying to forget him.'

' Are you aware that he's not engaged to Stephanie?'

' Yes, he told me. She's married to Eric.'

' When did he tell you?'

' In Capri. And it was easy to see how upset and unhappy he was.'

' Then he must have been upset about something else,'

Helen declared emphatically. 'Because he never was engaged to Stephanie.'

Melanie gave her mother a startled look. 'How do you know?'

'He told me. Now look, Melanie, it's high time you came to your senses. Drew is next door. He slept there last night on a camp bed. If you've any sense you'll go in there and somehow or other make him understand how you feel about him.'

Melanie shook her head quickly. 'But he's not in love with me. He had every chance to say so in Capri, but he didn't.'

Helen sighed and stood up. 'Melanie, don't you realise that first he thought you were in love with Eric, and then it appeared to be John? That's what he went to Naples to find out. I don't know what sort of impression you gave him, but if you don't do something you're going to lose him.'

'Lose him? But even if what you say is true—'

'I'm saying no more. I've probably said too much already. Just go in there tomorrow and at least find some way of letting him know that you're not engaged to John and have never been to Eric. It's worth a try—isn't it?'

'Yes, Mother, it is,' she answered quietly.

She scarcely dared hope too much, but after breakfast the following morning and wearing one of her most attractive trouser suits she went round to the rear door of his house, going through the large conservatory. She knocked on the door, but there was no response, so she pushed it open and went in. The room was devoid of furniture. She called out his name and listened, but at first all seemed quiet. Then as she moved towards the stair the sound of running water and the noise of splashing came to her ears. He was having a shower.

She moved from room to room. It was all exactly as she had designed it, and though the rooms had been decorated none had either carpets, curtains or furniture. Then she opened the last room on the ground floor and stood stock still. This was the only room which was furnished. It had a deep blue carpet, rich curtains in the same colour—and a grand piano.

Why?

She walked slowly across to the instrument and found it unlocked. She sat down on the long stool and began to play. The tone was beautiful. She did some improvisations, then drifted into Brahms' lullaby, the waltz from Coppélia, and into *Für Elise*. She did not hear Drew come into the room, but as the last notes died away she felt his hands on her neck as they had been that night in Capri.

'Melanie—'

She swung around and looked up at him. 'Drew—' she said, smiling up into his face. Then: 'You look—nice. And you smell nice, too.'

'Do I?' he asked in a strange voice.

She nodded. Fresh from his shower and smelling of some masculine toilet lotion, he was wearing a pair of velvet corduroy trousers in dark green, a short quilted jacket and a multi-coloured cravat at his throat.

'So this is what you look like in the mornings in your own home,' she said teasingly, though her heart was doing erratic gyrations.

'Sometimes,' he answered, looking at her with a strange questioning expression. 'Have you seen the rest of the rooms downstairs?'

She rose from the stool and stood facing him. 'Why no furniture yet, Drew—except for this room?'

'I took a chance on this room. I wanted at least one dream to—have some semblance of being realised. But the future of the house is really in the balance—and the balance is weighing heavily against me.'

She looked intently into his face. 'Drew, what do you mean?' she asked, her voice scarcely above a

186

whisper.

His hands came up to her shoulders. 'This house was designed and built for one person only.'

'Stephanie?' she ventured, in spite of what her mother had told her.

He shook his head. 'Stephanie—never. You, Melanie.'

'Drew!' she said on a swift intake of breath. 'Oh, Drew! Why didn't you tell me?'

Now there was no need to hide the joy exploded from within her and spilled out into her eyes and onto her face. She flung her arms around his neck as she had so often longed to do, and could have laughed aloud at the astonishment on his face.

'Melanie, you don't mean—'

'Drew, I love you, you—you dear, darling, silly man. I've loved you ever—'

But that was as far as she was allowed to go for the moment.

'Melanie—' he shouted joyfully. 'Oh, I can't believe it!'

He caught her in a hug which almost squeezed every ounce of breath from her body and kissed her as though he intended to go on doing it forever without ceasing. But at last he half released her and gave her a long, long look.

'Come over here,' he said, taking her by the hand, and leading her to the one armchair in the room, a comfortable, commodious, luxurious affair on which one could either sit, lie or recline. He sat down and pulled her on to his knee. 'Now then,' he began in an almost businesslike voice, 'let's get a few things straight. What about this career of yours?'

She leaned back in his arms and caressed his hair and letting her gaze dwell on his beloved features. 'Must we talk, darling, darling Drew?'

His expression softened. 'Sweetheart, I love you so

much. I can't begin to tell you—'

'We've got plenty of time, Drew,' she whispered. 'We've got the rest of our lives. I've got one or two professional engagements I must fulfil, then—no more.'

'Are you sure, darling?' he asked anxiously. 'I'd love to have you here at home, of course, but I wouldn't like to stand in your way if you—'

She shook her head. 'There'll be no American tour. One or two engagements a year, perhaps, or a charity concert or two, that's all. John—'

At the mention of John a small worried frown had appeared on his brow.

'Darling, was there ever anything—well, closer than friendship between you and John—or you and Eric?'

She shook her head. 'There was never, or ever will be, anyone else for me but you, John knows that. And I believe Eric knew it too.'

Drew's face clouded. 'For two pins I'd find our "friend" Eric and wring his insignificant little neck. He led me to believe—'

Melanie smoothed away the wrinkles from his brow. 'Well, maybe I'd like to do the same to Stephanie, but it's all in the past now, and besides, we won't have time. There's this house to furnish, carpets to buy—and oh, Drew, such a lot of lost time to make up for, such a lot of loving.'

He gave a long-drawn-out sigh and gathered her into his arms.

FREE! Harlequin Romance Catalogue

Here is a wonderful opportunity to read many of the Harlequin Romances you may have missed.

The HARLEQUIN ROMANCE CATALOGUE lists hundreds of titles which possibly are no longer available at your local bookseller. To receive your copy, just fill out the coupon below, mail it to us, and we'll rush your catalogue to you!

Following this page you'll find a sampling of a few of the Harlequin Romances listed in the catalogue. Should you wish to order any of these immediately, kindly check the titles desired and mail with coupon.

Have You Missed Any of These
Harlequin Romances?

- [ ] 1256 THE PINK JACARANDA
  Juliet Shore
- [ ] 1261 WITH ALL MY HEART
  Nan Asquith
- [ ] 1264 SECRET STAR
  Marguerite Lees
- [ ] 1270 THOUGH WORLDS APART
  Mary Burchell
- [ ] 1272 DEVON INTERLUDE
  Kay Thorpe
- [ ] 1274 MAN FROM THE SEA
  Pamela Kent
- [ ] 1275 SHAKE OUT THE STARS
  Janice Gray
- [ ] 1280 THE FLIGHT OF THE SWAN
  Eleanor Farnes
- [ ] 1282 THE SHINING STAR
  Hilary Wilde
- [ ] 1283 ROSALIND COMES HOME
  Essie Summers
- [ ] 1284 ONLY MY HEART TO GIVE
  Nan Asquith
- [ ] 1285 OUT OF A DREAM
  Jean Curtis
- [ ] 1286 BE MORE THAN DREAMS
  Elizabeth Hoy
- [ ] 1287 THE WALLED GARDEN
  Margaret Malcolm
- [ ] 1288 THE LAST OF THE KINTYRES
  Catherine Airlie
- [ ] 1290 A SUMMER TO LOVE
  Roumelia Lane
- [ ] 1291 MASTER OF GLENKEITH
  Jean S. Macleod
- [ ] 1293 I KNOW MY LOVE
  Sara Seale
- [ ] 1294 THE BREADTH OF HEAVEN
  Rosemary Pollock
- [ ] 1296 THE WIND AND THE SPRAY
  Joyce Dingwell
- [ ] 1299 THE LISTENING PALMS
  Juliet Shore
- [ ] 1301 HOTEL BY THE LOCH
  Iris Danbury
- [ ] 1303 STILL WATERS
  Marguerite Lees
- [ ] 1304 SHARLIE FOR SHORT
  Dorothy Rivers
- [ ] 1306 A HANDFUL OF SILVER
  Isobel Chace

- [ ] 1376 SHADOWS FROM THE SEA
  Jane Donnelly
- [ ] 1380 RELUCTANT MASQUERADE
  Henrietta Reid
- [ ] 1381 MUSIC ON THE WIND
  Dorothy Slide
- [ ] 1382 TO JOURNEY TOGETHER
  Mary Burchell
- [ ] 1383 A WIFE FOR ANDREW
  Lucy Gillen
- [ ] 1388 UNWARY HEART
  Anne Hampson
- [ ] 1389 MAN OF THE FOREST
  Hilda Pressley
- [ ] 1390 SUGAR IN THE MORNING
  Isobel Chace
- [ ] 1391 MY VALIANT FLEDGLING
  Margaret Malcolm
- [ ] 1392 THAT YOUNG PERSON
  Sara Seale
- [ ] 1395 TERMINUS TEHRAN
  Roumelia Lane
- [ ] 1396 BRIGHT WILDERNESS
  Gwen Westwood
- [ ] 1397 IF LOVE WERE WISE
  Elizabeth Hoy
- [ ] 1399 BLUE JASMINE
  Violet Winspear
- [ ] 1416 SUMMER IN DECEMBER
  Essie Summers
- [ ] 1421 PARISIAN ADVENTURE
  Elizabeth Ashton
- [ ] 1422 THE SOPHISTICATED URCHIN
  Rosalie Heneghan
- [ ] 1423 SULLIVAN'S REEF
  Anne Weale
- [ ] 1424 THE VENGEFUL HEART
  Roberta Leigh
- [ ] 1553 DOCTOR TOBY
  Lucy Gillen
- [ ] 1554 THE KEYS OF THE CASTLE
  Barbara Rowan
- [ ] 1555 RAINTREE VALLEY
  Violet Winspear
- [ ] 1556 NO ENEMY
  Hilda Nickson
- [ ] 1557 ALONG THE RIBBONWOOD
  TRACK   Mary Moore
- [ ] 1558 LEGEND OF ROSCANO
  Iris Danbury

All books listed are 50c.   Please use the handy order coupon.
D

L

M   GHL 972